The Pain of Love

To Andrea, Steve's profile appeared stern and unyielding. If he was remembering that kiss in Nogales—as she was—the memory wasn't bringing him any apparent enjoyment.

There was no reason to be miserable because one overbearing man was sending her away. Who would have believed that the prospect of leaving could hurt so much? Or that the memory of a kiss could still stir her senses hours later.

One tear slid down her face and was closely followed by another. She swallowed, being careful not to make a sound so that Steve wouldn't hear her. It was bad enough to be in love with him . . . she'd be darned if she'd give him concrete evidence.

When Love Speaks

by GLENNA FINLEY

A SIGNET BOOK

NEW AMERICAN LIBRARY

TIMES MIRROR

SIGNET, SIGNET CLASSICS, SIGNETTE, MENTOR AND PLUME BOOKS
are published by The New American Library, Inc.,
1301 Avenue of the Americas, New York, New York 10019

FIRST PRINTING, MAY, 1973

4 5 6 7 8 9

*And when Love speaks, the voice of all
    the gods
Makes heaven drowsy with the harmony.*

—William Shakespeare

Chapter ONE

"Will Miss Andrea Sinclair check in at the ticket window, please. Miss Andrea Sinclair."

The impersonal voice crackled over the public-address system in Tucson's railroad depot and out to the loading platforms beyond. It was only nine o'clock in the morning, but the July sun beat down with smothering intensity on the concrete apron by the tracks, where an attractive young woman sat atop her suitcases, fanning herself with yesterday's Los Angeles newspaper.

As the announcement was repeated, she said, "Well, finally," and stood up. Then she stared irritably down at the heavy suitcases and shifted her camel's hair topcoat on her arm. She was already wishing she could throttle the well-meaning friend who had advised bringing the coat.

"So it gets cold at night," she murmured as she gave it another despairing glance and felt the perspiration trickling down her arm. "At this rate, I'll keel over from heat prostration before noon." She looked around, then leaned over and dropped the coat on the suitcases—obviously no one in his right mind would take it, even if she had it gift-wrapped. Unencumbered, she strolled toward the terminal.

More than one interested masculine glance followed her progress. Size ten, brown-eyed blonds with trim ankles and admirable knees have a way of attracting attention even when the thermometer hovers at ninety-two degrees.

By the time Andrea reached the station, her temperature registered considerably higher. She swept through the room and up to the ticket window. "I'm Miss Sinclair," she informed the mild-looking clerk. "Was there a message for me?"

He blinked once and then again. "That's right, miss. Fellow over there in the corner's waiting for you." He nodded toward a man wearing jeans and a tan work shirt who was leaning against the wall watching their discussion with calm amusement.

Andrea surveyed his tall figure deliberately in turn. He was about six feet, with features that indicated Nordic ancestry not too far back. His hair was fair, cut conservatively short, and bleached almost white by the sun, which made the leathery tan on his face startling by contrast. The network of fine wrinkles at the corners of his eyes and around a firm mouth belied her initial impression of youth. Taking a second look, she concluded he must be in his early thirties, at least. Despite the added years, there wasn't a spare ounce of flesh on his waistline, and the faded jeans fitted trimly around slim hips. He stood easily under her scrutiny, but there was an impression of leashed strength beneath the repose. Slowly her appraising glance moved upward to his face.

A pair of sleepy blue eyes stared steadily back at her. Then—deliberately, it seemed—he yawned, and his hand was slow in coming up to stifle it.

The gesture made Andrea seethe. No wonder he was late in meeting her. Probably he'd been partying the night before and simply couldn't get out of bed on time. A closer look bolstered her suspicions. His eyes were red-rimmed with fatigue. Some introduction to the romantic Southwest! Her first cowboy, and he obviously needed two aspirin and eight hours' sleep.

"Miss Sinclair?" His tone was deep but noncommittal. "My name's York. . . . Steve York. Graham Brinkley, the manager out at the ranch, asked me to meet you."

"I gathered that," she said carefully. Although they hadn't moved, Andrea felt that they were circling, stiff-legged, like two strange terriers. "I'm ready to go when you are. I have been . . . for some time." She noted with satisfaction the sudden surge of red under his cheekbones.

"Er . . . yes. I'm sorry." His words came out with difficulty. "I guess I was a little late."

"The train," she pointed out, "was a little early."

His thick eyebrows rose. "Trains are never early."

"This one was." She was leading the way to her luggage as she spoke. "It happens all the time these days. The conductor said it was part of Amtrak's new scheduling."

8

"I'll remember." His drawl had a definite bite now. As they went out in the sunshine, he settled a dusty white Stetson squarely on his head. "Not many of our guests come by train. Mostly we meet them at the airport."

"Then I hope they have the good sense to pick an afternoon plane," she said sweetly. It had been a long wait on the platform, and this . . . Steve York . . . certainly wasn't overcome with remorse.

He didn't deign to reply. Instead, he merely nodded to the pile of luggage in front of them. "These yours?"

"That's right." As he stooped to retrieve her coat, she added hurriedly, "I'll take that."

"Yes, ma'am."

He started to unfold it, but she snatched it from his hands. "I don't want to wear it, for heaven's sake. What do you think I am?"

"I couldn't say, Miss Sinclair." He didn't give her time to reflect on that. "The car's parked right along here. You can follow me." Without looking around, he strode through a brick archway to the side of the terminal.

Andrea had to hurry to keep him in sight. By the time she caught up with him at the curb, perspiration mirrored her forehead, and the coat over her arm felt like a sealskin parka.

Steve was calmly stowing her bags in a dusty green station wagon which bore a replica of the Circle C brand on the front door. After he'd slammed the tailgate, he came around to pointedly open the second door of the wagon for her.

She glanced at the empty front seat and felt her cheeks grow even more fiery, but she stepped in where he indicated. Unfortunately she caught her heel in the hem of her coat as she went.

"Damn!" As she struggled to sit upright, there was a suspicious choking sound behind her. She glared over her shoulder, but by then Steve's expression was as impassive as ever.

"Would you like me to take that coat, ma'am?"

"No, thank you. I can manage." She shoved it down to the end of the seat, wishing she could shove it into the nearest litter barrel instead. "It will probably come in handy. I was told that it gets cool here after the sun goes down."

"Yes, ma'am." He closed the car door.

She waited until he'd backed out of the parking space and turned into the street before she went on. "How hot was it here yesterday?"

He didn't turn his head. "A hundred and twelve, ma'am."

"Oh." She digested that for a long city block and wished he'd stop calling her "ma'am" every time he opened his mouth. "What about the nighttime temperature?"

"Eighty four . . . ma'am."

That time he tacked it on deliberately, she was sure. Her frowning glance went from the back of his neck to the rear-vision mirror, and she found herself staring into those blue eyes once again. She noted that they were no longer sleepy, but brimming with laughter.

Hastily she glanced out the side window and tried to focus on the buildings of downtown Tucson. If she could only go back and start over again. Nothing had gone right since she'd heard about this trip in Los Angeles a week ago. That was when her chief in the Foreign Visitors Bureau had decided that Andrea should familiarize herself with western-style dude ranches.

"It's amazing how many Europeans want to get a look at a real cowboy," he'd told her. "You'd better check one out."

"But I don't know a darned thing about guest ranches," she had protested.

"That's just the point. Somebody in this office should," he said sternly. "We've forty-five Germans coming on that bus tour next month, and two coachfuls of Japanese arriving three weeks from now. Both groups have indicated an interest in cowboys and the wide-open spaces. Comes from watching all those television programs, I suppose. You'd better go to Tucson and see what a dude ranch is really like. There's a brochure around here somewhere from the Circle C. . . ." He fumbled among the papers on the top of his desk and then waved a brightly colored folder triumphantly. "Here it is."

"I saw it," she said with a feeling of foreboding. "But Tucson in July?"

"What's wrong with that? We can't wait . . . our visitors don't," he added. "I'd hate to have our directors getting complaints about the resorts we're recommending."

10

Andrea knew when she was beaten. "Yes, sir. Shall I call for reservations right away?"

"Of course, dear girl." He put the brochure in her unwilling hands.

"How long do I stay?"

"A week should be enough. I need you back here when I leave for my vacation."

Her interest flickered. "So you settled on someplace to go?"

"My wife did," he mumbled. "She's signed up for a two-week nature ride on horseback."

"Horseback?" Andrea paused by his office door with a sudden spurt of hope. "Maybe she'd like to try a guest ranch. . . ."

"She would . . . in Wyoming. We can compare notes with you after we've returned. Be sure and take the right clothing—you have to make allowances for weather changes. I've heard it gets cold there at night."

Andrea's eyebrows settled in an ominous line at that memory. Cold indeed! Like Death Valley at high noon. She sighed softly. The train trip had been his brilliant idea too. "Better go Amtrak," he'd written in a memo. Andrea's desk was thick with memos. "Remember how many foreign visitors want to try American trains. Let's avoid any more fiascos like the one with that Yugoslavian woman last month. Her husband is still complaining and writing letters."

"There was nothing wrong with the compartment I reserved for her," Andrea had said defensively when she cornered him at the water cooler.

His nose twitched. "Not much. It only had one berth, didn't it?"

"But no one told me that she was traveling with her three children."

"All under six," he went on relentlessly. "The Yugoslavian embassy told *me* fast enough the next morning. God! I hope that doesn't happen again. When you're on the train to Tucson, make a memo on the dimensions of those sleeping rooms."

She had planned to obey. It wasn't her fault that she'd gotten in the wrong car at the station in Los Angeles. By the time she'd been directed to the proper space, she was so tired she'd simply lowered her berth and gone to

11

sleep. That was why she hadn't noticed the faulty window shade until the next morning. It had slipped quietly upward while she was washing her face at the tiny basin, and she'd turned around, half-dressed, to receive a battery of amused glances from the train crew working on the platform at Phoenix. Feeling a complete fool, she'd yanked the curtain down and completed dressing posthaste. No wonder the men used to come down to the station and watch the trains go by! She should have charged admission.

A well-served breakfast in the diner restored some of her morale. At least she'd enjoyed watching the bright green fields of cotton flash by on either side of the train. The lush foliage was interspersed with acres of dry Arizona grazing land, which appeared desolate by contrast. In the distance, craggy purple-gray mountains rimmed the valley, their sharp outlines softened by the haze that hung about them. The closer foothills bristled with saguaro cactus, which resembled stubbly chin whiskers on rounded rock faces. As the train continued southward, the more jagged the stone profiles became.

When Andrea stepped off the Pullman in Tucson, she found the mountains weren't the only things that had gotten steeper; the temperature had risen as well. By the time Steve York had finally appeared, she was so exhausted by the heat that she would have quarreled with St. Peter if he'd tried to usher her into heaven.

She was heartily regretting her words now that the air-conditioner in the station wagon was making itself felt. Maybe Steve did have a logical excuse for being late. At least she should have let him explain. She brought her gaze reluctantly back to the front of the car.

He must have been watching, because he suddenly said, "Those red brick buildings on the right belong to the University of Arizona . . . or do you know Tucson?"

She decided it was time for an olive branch. "Would anybody who knew Tucson bring a topcoat in July?"

Their glances met again momentarily in the rear-vision mirror.

"I've heard—on the best authority—that it sometimes turns cold at night on the desert," he said softly. "Most women don't show such foresight."

"Right now I'd trade the foresight for better manners,"

12

she admitted as he pulled up at a traffic light and half-turned in the seat to survey her. "I'm sorry I was so unpleasant at the station. Put it down to a combination of things."

He grinned. "That's all right. I didn't mean to be late, either. The morning wasn't exactly great at the ranch. . . ." The blast of a horn from the car behind them made him turn around and accelerate rapidly. "Sorry. I guess I'm still behind schedule." He was peering thrugh the windshield to the right as he spoke. "I'm meeting a fellow from the Circle C at a restaurant up the street here. Maybe you'd like to join us for a cup of coffee. Unless you'd prefer going on to the ranch and having some there," he added politely.

"A cup of coffee sounds just right," she said, relieved that her peace feeler had been accepted, and surprised to find how pleasant an Arizona cowhand could be if he set his mind to it.

"Fine. There's the place in the next block—next to the shopping center." He swung the wagon into the slow lane of the street and then turned off into a large parking lot. Threading through the cars, he was able to find an empty slot next to an attractive coffee shop. He braked and shut off the ignition before taking off his hat and tossing it on the seat. "You can leave your stuff in the car," he told Andrea. "I'll be locking it, so there's no point in struggling."

"You don't have to convince me. It would be wonderful if you could travel with just a toothbrush." She slid down to the end of the seat and fumbled with the catch on her door.

"Just a minute . . . I'll get that," he said, moving over and grabbing the door handle.

"Thanks." She stood beside the car smoothing the skirt of her leaf-green shirtwaist. Fortunately the dress still looked crisp, even though the air felt as if someone had opened an oven door nearby. Andrea pushed back a strand of hair from her forehead and gave silent thanks that she'd pulled the rest into a cool ponytail style.

Steve surveyed her movements with quiet amusement. "You'll feel better when you get inside. All the eating places here are air-conditioned."

She fell in beside him. "I should have carried some

sort of hat. You'd think I'd have known, after living in Los Angeles."

He held the restaurant door for her and said, "This desert heat's a little different. You'll like it, though, once you get used to it."

"Ummm . . . I like this at any rate." She was looking around the interior of the restaurant with approval. Used brick on the walls and an indoor fountain surrounded by greenery in the center of the room provided an informal charm.

"It's buffet service at this time of day," Steve said. "You pick a table, and I'll get our coffee."

"What about your friend?"

"Guess he hasn't shown yet. Don't worry—he'll be along. Juan's not one to miss a cup of coffee."

She watched him stroll off to the far side of the restaurant, and turned to select a table near the fountain and surrounding pool. Fat, orange carp swam lazily in the shallow water, obviously content with their lot in life.

Steve came back soon carrying a tray laden with an insulated coffee server, mugs, and a plate of bran muffins. "I hope you're hungry," he said as he sorted it out on the table. "Breakfast at the ranch was a long time ago."

"You mean you were up for breakfast?" The surprised remark came out before she had time to think.

"Naturally." His eyebrows drew together as he peered at her. "What did you think? That I just rolled out of the sack in time to be late for the train?"

His astuteness made her wince. "Something like that. It's the story of my life." She watched him stifle a yawn as he poured their coffee. "You really are short on sleep, aren't you?"

"Coffee will help." He sounded like a man who wanted to change the subject. "How about a muffin?"

"No, thanks—this coffee's enough. Do you usually have to work such long hours at the ranch? I thought this was off-season."

"It is, but the work goes on the year round. We have more maintenance in the summer to get the horses and gear in shape for winter visitors."

"I see." As he swallowed a bite of muffin and took a sip of coffee, she went on. "If it's that much responsi-

14

bility, the manager should hire some more help. Have you asked him?"

"Whoa there. Things aren't this bad all the time." He pushed back in his chair slightly. "Last night was worse than usual."

"Oh?" Andrea was all attention. "What happened?"

"I was sitting up with a sick horse," he said tersely. "Would you like a cigarette?"

"No, thanks." She watched him take one from the package in his shirt pocket and light it with an economy of movement. His muscular forearms looked teak-colored against his tan shirt as he folded them across his chest and stared at her. Disconcerted by that steady gaze, she asked confusedly, "Did it get better?"

"What?"

"The sick horse."

"Oh . . . sure thing. Improved a hundred percent."

"That's good." She beamed. "What was wrong with it?"

He transferred his glance to the end of his cigarette. "Nothing too bad . . . a pulled muscle mainly. Look"—he pushed the muffin plate toward her—"are you sure you don't want something to eat?"

"Quite sure. How did you happen to become a cowboy, Mr. York?"

He started to laugh. "You'd better make it 'Steve' if this is the biographical quiz. Tell me one thing first— do all of your sentences end with question marks?"

She sat back, embarrassed. "Sorry, I didn't mean to cross-examine you. It's just that these things . . ."—she made an airy gesture,—"guest ranches and wranglers and horses are all new to me. You can put it down to excitement."

"Believe me, lady, cleaning out the corral on a hot afternoon is hardly exciting."

Her chin firmed. "You know what I mean."

"Of course I do, but you shouldn't believe all those television programs."

"I'd still like to know how you became a cowboy."

He looked mildly irritated. "And I wish you'd use another word. You make me feel I should be carrying a git-tar, rolling my own cigarettes, and heading for the pass to cut off the cavalry."

"Don't be silly. Even I'm not as naïve about cowboys

15

. . . er . . . the people who work on the Circle C as all that. I just wondered what kind of a background cowboys . . . I mean, wranglers have."

"You don't have to invent another word. 'Cowboy' still gets the message across," he told her. "I'll stop being so stiff-necked. If you really want to know, most people in my line of business grew up on a ranch. In my case, it was Colorado. My dad still has a spread there."

"Then this kind of job has been your life?"

"You could say that." He poured more coffee absently. "I'm curious now. What made you come to the Circle C?"

"My job depended on it," she confessed, and went on to tell him the reason for her research. "So you see," she said, finishing, "I have to learn everything about the Southwest in one fast week. Then I can answer questions like 'Should I pack spurs in my suitcase?' and 'Will I need a topcoat when it gets cold at night?'"

He chuckled. "You've learned the answer to that one already. As for the rest, Graham can give you all the information you'll need."

"Graham?"

"The resident manager, Graham Brinkley. Very good at his job. He's been at the Circle C for a couple of years."

She sipped her coffee. "Then I'll make him my listening post. Now that I know you're allergic to questions, I'll need other sources."

Steve ignored her teasing. "You could ask Françoise or Roger Villier. They run the guest shop and stay in the thick of things."

"They sound awfully French."

"All the way." Steve ground out his cigarette in the ashtray. "From Marseilles, I believe. Roger,"—he gave the name a French pronunciation—"has a U.S. work permit, but Françoise just came over last month with a tourist's visa."

Andrea was puzzled. "That doesn't sound like a good basis for marriage, but maybe it's the European way of doing things."

"Even Europeans aren't keen on having the Atlantic Ocean between them," Steve said, smiling. "Françoise and Roger are simply cousins—marriage doesn't come into it. He's busy teaching her the retail business, and she

16

also works as the ranch swimming instructor when she's not in the shop."

"That's not all she does," said a voice behind them. "In her off-hours, she helps improve French-American relations."

Steve glanced around at the interruption and then half-rose to push back another chair at their table. "I wondered when you were going to show. Miss Sinclair . . . this is Juan Núñez. He's at the Circle C, too."

"How do you do," Andrea said as the newcomer nodded easily and sat down beside them. One hasty glance convinced her that Arizona ranch hands came in all shapes and sizes. Other than these two being dressed almost identically, there wasn't any resemblance at all.

Juan was barely above medium height, and stockily built. His impression of ruggedness stopped at his broad shoulders, as his facial characteristics were finely drawn and exceptionally handsome. Jet black hair just touched his collar, but it was combed severely back from his face to reveal prominent cheekbones and an aquiline nose which must have been a throwback to Aztec chieftains. His deep-set dark eyes gleamed with interest as he surveyed her.

"Glad to know you, Miss Sinclair. If I'd realized our new guest was going to look like you, I'd have been here earlier."

"Juan isn't the greatest on a horse," Steve pointed out dryly, "but he's very popular with the ladies at Circle C."

"Pay no attention," the other told her. "He's just jealous. What comes before 'Sinclair'?"

Andrea pressed her lips together to keep from laughing. Juan couldn't have been older than twenty-five—just as she was—but his technique was pleasantly experienced. His dark glance was brimming with amusement as he waited for her answer. She decided to hold him off. "Usually just 'Miss,'" she proclaimed gravely, "but I answer to most anything."

"So do I," he admitted. "Don't you think I'd better hurry and catch up, though? Steve's already one cup of coffee ahead of me."

"He's still at the 'Miss Sinclair' stage, too," she said. "If you're really worried about catching up, my first name's 'Andrea'."

17

"Andrea . . ." It was given a soft, south-of-the-border pronunciation. "Very nice." He nodded his thanks as Steve pushed a mug of coffee toward him. "Does anybody call you 'Andy'?" he asked her slyly.

"Not more than once."

Steve's glance came up. "Don't you like the nickname?"

"I'd have to be so besotted with the man that I'd lost my reason. Happily, that state of affairs hasn't occurred yet, but I'd be pleased if you'd both call me 'Andrea'." An elusive dimple flickered in her cheek. "I left 'Miss Sinclair' in the station wagon along with my coat, and I don't plan to resurrect either of them until I go home again."

"Olé!" Juan raised his coffee in salute. "The dude-ranch business is looking up, and frankly, it's about time. I was ready to give it a miss."

"Isn't ranching a life's work with you?" she asked.

Juan shrugged. "It's a living. Who's out for a career? When I get tired, I'll go home."

"And where's that?"

"El Paso . . . for the last generation or so. Most of my relatives still live in Chihuahua. You could fill an auditorium with the Núñez family, but we're the rich branch of the family."

"Oh?"

He nodded solemnly. "Chicken every Sunday."

"Plus a brilliant son named Juan who only has two more payments on his sports car," Steve finished for him.

"Exactly." The younger man turned to Andrea. "A real American success story. Right? How would you like to take a ride with me on my night off? For you . . . I'll drive very carefully."

"Check with your insurance man first," Steve told her in his slow drawl. " 'Carefully' to Juan means anything under sixty."

Juan shrugged again. "A man has to have some fun in life. I don't like working all the time."

The mild complaint didn't bother Steve. He merely said, "I gather you weren't able to round up any more help for us."

"You gather right, my friend." Juan turned his attention to Andrea. "What about our date? I'm off tomorrow night."

18

She smiled. "Let's wait and see. Maybe you should bring along a safe-driving certificate first."

"Oh, that." Juan snapped his fingers. "Steve fusses too much. Comes from working too hard."

"And sitting up with sick horses like last night," Andrea added sympathetically. "It really does sound as if you could use more help on the ranch. Look, maybe I could say something about it casually . . . when I talk to the manager."

"I don't think you'd better," Steve began.

"You needn't worry that I'd involve you two in any way. Don't you think it's a good idea, Juan?"

"Sitting up with sick horses . . ." he muttered.

"I beg your pardon," Andrea said, puzzled.

"Miss Sinclair's asking you a question, Juan," Steve cut in. "Come to the party."

"Sorry. I was thinking of something else."

"She was offering to put some pressure on Graham, but I told her we'd manage."

"Oh, sure thing. Steve's right, Andrea. We do fine most of the time. You just caught us a little off-base today —with the sick livestock and all. Isn't that right, amigo?" He turned his solemn glance toward Steve.

"Absolutely," the other assured him, "and don't you forget it."

"Well, you've lost me." Andrea's tone was bewildered.

Juan grinned at her as he broke a piece off the last muffin and swung around in his chair. "Come on, let's give these fish a handout. They're positively starving to death."

She bent over to stare at fat orange stomachs. "They're so fat they can hardly wriggle now," she corrected. "Are muffins on their diet list?"

"Bran muffins every Thursday morning," he intoned, handing her a crumb. "The one over at the left is your responsibility."

Steve took a final sip of coffee and watched them morosely. This morning, more than ever, the ten years difference in age between him and Juan was making itself felt. The younger man hadn't any more sleep than he the night before, but Juan didn't look as if he'd missed a wink. Of course, a pretty girl could always raise the Núñez pulse rate, and Andrea Sinclair certainly came under that cate-

19

gory. With that ridiculous ponytail bobbing on the back of her head, she looked about fifteen years old. His glance swept beyond her graceful throat and shoulders to note the soft curve of her breast under the thin dress material, and his eyes became thoughtful slits. That tantalizing silhouette didn't belong to a fifteen-year-old, he decided reluctantly. Neither did her assured manner or the soft voice that could firm with determination. The way she had flared at him in the railroad station reminded him of a Yorkshire terrier with teeth bared under a dainty ribbon topknot. Only a fool, he reminded himself, would ignore the growl despite the attractive outer trappings. Andrea Sinclair was decorative—damned decorative; no one could dispute that. But right now he just didn't have time to play. It was a pity, but that's the way it was. If she wanted masculine diversion at the Circle C, Juan and probably Graham himself would be happy to oblige.

He pushed back his chair and sighed so audibly that both Juan and Andrea glanced his way.

"Want to be going, Steve?" the younger man asked.

"We'd better. Do you care for anything else, Miss Sinclair?"

Andrea noted his determination to remain formal and decided perversely to override it. "I'm ready, but could you please drop the 'Miss Sinclair'? 'Andrea' will do fine if you don't mind . . . Steve." Her look was unconsciously provocative, the inference obvious that she usually didn't bother with such requests.

"Whatever you say." His response was grudging as he led the way to the door. "Will you drive, Juan? Andrea can sit beside you and have a guided tour on the way to the ranch." He opened the car door for her. "I'll sit in back this time."

"Surely there's enough room in the front for three of us." She hesitated before sliding along the wide seat.

He urged her in. "No point in being crowded in this weather. Besides, I can catch a nap on the way home. We still have fifteen miles or so."

Juan got in on the driver's side and slammed his door. "Do that, my friend. It was a hard night."

"Ummm." Steve's reply was muffled. He closed the door behind Andrea and got in the rear seat without further comment.

She allowed herself one quick look over her shoulder as they drove out of the parking lot. He had already slouched against the side of the car and closed his eyes.

Evidently she hadn't made much of an impression on the man, she decided irritably. For a few minutes after they'd arrived at the restaurant his reaction was quite different. There had been a definite current of understanding between them. Then, deliberately, he'd simply closed her out, and they were back at square one.

Andrea gave a mental shrug. If that was the way Mr. York wanted it, she certainly wouldn't bother to change his mind. Craggy cowhands weren't her type, anyhow. What would they talk about once they'd exhausted the symptoms of hoof-and-mouth disease? She ignored the fact that it wasn't Steve York's conversational technique that had interested her in the first place. Hardly. Not if she were honest with herself—the man's rugged features and taciturn manner gave him an understated sex appeal that would fascinate any woman. She turned to stare out the window as her thoughts raced onward.

". . . Originally this was all desert, but now the developers have taken over, and they're fighting with the Park Service for any available land." Juan's voice was on the fringe of her consciousness. "The acreage you see on those Rincon foothills over to the right is all a National Monument. The Circle C has the right to use the land for riding, so long as we don't disturb any of the natural terrain. Nice, huh?"

Andrea blinked, trying to sort out his remark. She'd hate to admit that her mind had been far beyond the roadside scenery. "Very nice," she murmured finally. "I didn't know there were so many shapes and sizes of cactus."

"They all have one thing in common." It was the lazy voice from the back seat.

"Oh?" She was cool as she acknowledged it. "And what's that?"

Juan answered first. "Spines, Andrea. Fall off your horse, and it's like landing in a porcupine convention. Isn't that right, Steve?"

"Precisely. But maybe Andrea can take care of herself and doesn't have to worry about that." Steve could hear the derisive note in his own voice and wished that

21

he'd kept quiet in the first place. He'd planned to ignore the woman, and now he was climbing into the fray just like Juan.

"How about it, Andrea?" The younger man was obviously enjoying the teasing.

She was torn between a desire to tell the truth and yet keep her dignity in front of Steve. Eventually she compromised, saying, "It's been several years since I was on a horse." There was no point in adding that her experience had consisted of a half-hour ride on the beach one weekend.

"Never mind. It's like riding a bicycle . . . it all comes back to you," Juan said comfortingly. "Besides, we have some gentle mounts. There are lots of people like you who stay at guest ranches."

"The list grows longer every day," Steve confirmed.

Andrea was stung by that bored tone. "I'll try not to cause you any trouble," she told him.

"I don't expect you to cause me any trouble at all," Steve replied, irritated in turn. She could interpret that comment any way she chose. He slouched down again and deliberately pulled the brim of his hat over his forehead, silencing the conversation.

When the split-rail gate of the Circle C came into view a little later, Andrea roused herself to stare at the cluster of buildings on the hillside.

"This looks like a complete town," she said to Juan. "Are all those buildings part of the ranch?"

He nodded as he slowed the station wagon over the dusty ruts of the road. "That long one with the porch contains the office and a few of the single guest rooms. The dining hall's over to the right. Beyond that, you'll find the gift shop. On the other side, the low building is attached to the corral." He looked in the rear-vision mirror. "Want me to drop you there, Steve?"

"No, thanks. I'll go on to the office with you. There are a couple of things I want to ask Graham."

"Okay." Juan turned left onto the drive circling a patch of lawn in front of the main building. "Those separate houses on the hillside," he told Andrea, "are individual chalets for guests who want their own quarters and patios. All air-conditioned, with phones . . . room service . . . the works."

"Just bring money," she replied, smiling.

He grinned back at her. "That's the girl. You've hit the magic word. Once you've paid the tariff at the Circle C, your wish is our command. Horses, cowhands, swimming lessons in the indoor or outdoor pool, cookouts on the trail . . . snap your fingers and we come running."

"All of you?"

"Not quite," Steve said flatly. "Juan's pulling your leg a little, Miss Sinclair. Naturally we do our best to send everybody away satisfied. Stop here in front of the office, Juan," he added before she could reply.

"Right." Juan braked by the deep-shaded porch. There was a mini-garden by the screen door leading to the office, which contained a tall saguaro, a plump barrel cactus, and a prickly pear. White rock chips covered their roots in an attractive arrangement. "Welcome to the Circle C, Andrea," Juan said. "Come along, and I'll introduce you to our manager. I'll probably have to pull him out of the library. He usually has coffee in there about this time. Graham would rather read a book than run a ranch any day. Naturally most of us are all in favor of his hobby; it doesn't leave him much time to ride herd on us."

"What hobby is that?" Andrea asked, trailing him to the front door. From the corner of her eye, she noticed Steve falling behind to speak to someone.

"Indian artifacts of the Southwest." Juan held open the door and waved toward the office interior. "See what I mean? This looks like the wing of a museum."

Andrea stepped inside and then stopped in surprise. Shelves full of religious plaques and ancient clay pots lined the walls of the tiny room. The registration counter and cashier's window over in one corner were obviously an afterthought.

As she stood there, a muscular-looking man in his early forties came through a door at the rear of the office. Thick, prematurely gray hair was brushed neatly back from a scholar's forehead, and his alert gray eyes went over her in flattering detail. She noted that his pleasant face was deeply tanned, as were the powerful forearms revealed by his short-sleeved twill shirt.

"Miss Sinclair? I'm Graham Brinkley, the manager here. Welcome to the Circle C. . . ." He held out a hand as he spoke and took hers in a firm grip. "I've wanted to say

23

'thank you' to the Foreign Visitors Bureau for a long time. You've sent us a lot of guests, and we do appreciate it." Her face must have shown her lingering surprise at the office furnishing because he added genially, "Juan should have warned you about my collecting habits. The trouble is, I've just plain run out of shelves in my bedroom and the lounge."

"It all looks very interesting," she said, recovering somewhat.

"Not unless you're immersed in early Southwest history the way I am. Don't worry, Andrea . . . may I call you 'Andrea'?" He barely waited for her dazed nod. "Early Indian history isn't a requirement here. All we ask at the Circle C is that you have a good time." He held out a pen for her to register, adding, "Juan and Steve help take care of that part." Then, glancing around as if just aware that something was missing, he asked, "Where is Steve?"

"Outside . . . talking to somebody, I guess." Juan went over by the screen door and listened. He turned back. "Françoise . . . naturally."

"Naturally," Graham said wryly. He picked up Andrea's completed registration card, and his expression lightened as he scanned its particulars. "Fine . . . fine. By the way, my dear, you *do* ride, don't you?"

"Sure she does," Juan cut in. "We've already asked her."

"Good." The manager tucked the card in a drawer. "Then she can join Steve on the four-o'clock ride this afternoon. Unfortunately, it's too late to join the morning one."

"I don't mind a bit," Andrea said truthfully.

Graham was fumbling for a small printed card, which he presented to her along with a door key. "Here's a listing of our mealtimes. You can meet the other guests at lunch. In the meantime, you'd probably like a dip in the pool. This desert temperature is a little overpowering until you're used to it."

She gave him a dazed look. The temperature wasn't the only thing that was overpowering; Graham himself exuded so much energy that he made her feel like a hibernating sloth. It was hard to connect that dynamic masculine personality of his with the study of Indian archaeology.

"Françoise Villier will assist you if you'd like any instruction in the pool," he was going on. "We're lucky to have her. Actually, she holds several French aquatic championships, but she's visiting here to help her cousin for the summer. He runs the ranch gift shop." Graham patted her shoulder. "I mustn't tell you any more or I'll have you completely confused. Juan, take Andrea up to cottage twelve, please."

"O.K., boss. Come on, Andrea. We'll go in the wagon and take the back way. There's no need for you to walk up the path." He held the door for her.

Graham followed them to the screen. "I meant to tell you that coffee's always available in the dining room between meals. Any of the waitresses will be glad to show you."

She smiled over her shoulder. "That sounds wonderful. Thank you, Mr. Brinkley."

" 'Graham,' my dear. Formality is the one thing our guests are told to leave at home." His tone was avuncular. "Let me know if there's anything I can do to make your stay more pleasant."

"Thanks, I will." She nodded and turned to follow Juan. There was no need for Graham Brinkley to be quite so effusive, she was thinking as she took the path to the drive. Of course, lots of resort managers were that way, and she'd dealt with enough to realize that affability was a prime asset. She made a careful detour around the cactus garden, sticking to the far side of the gravel footpath.

"Bonjour, Françoise. Comment allez-vous? Juan said easily as he pulled up by the station wagon ahead of her.

A strikingly pretty brunette wearing a blue body shirt and hip-hugging jeans was leaning against the car talking to Steve in the driver's seat. She glanced at the newcomers without appreciable interest. " '*Jour*, Juan." Andrea's presence was dismissed with a casual look before she bent her attention to Steve once more.

Andrea felt her cheeks redden. Not all the staff at the Circle C was as welcoming as Graham Brinkley, it seemed. Françoise must have been taking lessons in guest-baiting from Steve.

She surveyed the two of them uncertainly, still unsure of what to do. Juan solved the dilemma. He swept open the rear door and gestured for her to get in.

"I'm instructed to take Andrea to number twelve," he said.

"I'll drive you up," Steve said casually.

"Okay, then I'll ride by our guest of honor." Juan squeezed in beside her. "Oh, I'm sorry, Andrea . . . you haven't officially met Françoise Villier. She's on the staff here, too. Françoise, this is Miss Andrea Sinclair."

"How do you do," Andrea murmured.

The Frenchwoman stared into the back seat while brushing back a strand of hair which had escaped from her stylish gamine cut. Smooth olive skin, soulful dark eyes, and high cheekbones gave her the appearance of a model from a Parisian boutique.

Her response held a European directness. "Why 'ave you come to thees place, Mees Sinclair? There ees nothing to interest you."

"Watch it, Françoise." Surprisingly, it was Steve's warning.

"Don't be angry, *mon cher.*" She placed a graceful hand on his shoulder. "I meant it as a compliment. You know the kind of American woman that comes here—like old Madame Carter and 'er 'orrible granddaughter. All they think about is 'orses."

Françoise's struggle with her *h*'s drew both men's attention to her beautifully shaped lips, Andrea noticed. Was it deliberate, or purely by accident?

"Mees Sinclair ees not the type for 'orses. Are you, *mademoiselle?*"

Andrea kept her expression solemn. "Actually, I'm more impressed with your cowboys."

Françoise hadn't mastered American humor. She frowned. "Then you are wasting your time unless you like Graham or my cousin Roger. The rest of them are . . ."—her palms came up in a Gallic gesture—"how do you say it . . . ?"

"Taken? Already reserved? *Mieux vaut tard que jamais,*" Andrea said easily. "Thanks for the warning, though. I'll make a note of it." No wonder the French had needed a Maginot Line to defend themselves if their citizens were like this woman! Françoise could start a revolution all by herself.

Steve must have been reading her mind again, because

26

he switched on the ignition key. "We'd better be going. See you later, Françoise."

"Soon, Steve?" She sounded as if she wouldn't breathe until he returned.

"As soon as I deposit Miss Sinclair and her things."

Françoise was evidently reassured. She leaned in the window and purred, *"Au revoir, mademoiselle.* We'll meet at lunch or in the pool, perhaps."

Andrea smiled thinly. In that case, she'd stay out of the deep end.

Just then Françoise caught sight of the camel's hair topcoat piled on the suitcases. "What ees that?" she asked in strident tones. "You didn't bring a coat with you? Not 'ere . . . to the desert?"

It was a wonder she didn't ring cowbells or send up rockets; nothing could have made Andrea feel more of a fool. Desperately she searched for an answer . . . any answer. "It does look strange," she found herself responding, "but it's actually a long story. When I represented Iceland in the Miss Universe contest last month, I had to follow the pageant rules on clothing."

Françoise's eyes widened. "Miss Universe? Iceland?"

"Uh-huh. You see, in cold countries they don't allow swimsuits for the tryouts, so I just had my sealskin parka and this camel's hair coat. Unfortunately, my money ran out after the finals, and I lost my ticket back to Reykjavik, so I came to the Circle C in hopes I could . . ."

Steve gunned the motor noisily, cutting her off in midsentence as he wheeled the station wagon out of the drive with a snap that sprayed gravel behind them.

Juan was doubled over with laughter. "Miss Iceland! Boy—when Françoise figures that one out, you'll be dead in the water. She hasn't much of a sense of humor anytime, but today, after being up most of last night partying with Steve . . ." His voice trailed off as his gaffe registered.

Other than a muffled epithet from the front seat, Steve's only visible reaction was to grip the steering wheel like a vise as the car followed the winding hillside track above the main ranch buildings.

Andrea was suddenly so mad that she could have thrown anything at the back of that stolid sandy head. So he was sitting up with a sick horse, was he! And she'd fallen for the hoary joke like the greenest dude imaginable.

27

Not only that, she'd apologized for her bad temper after he'd left her sitting in the sun while he probably nursed a hangover. It was a darned shame that the Navajos hadn't beaten the cavalry a hundred years ago and roasted some of Mr. York's ancestors at the stake!

Aloud she managed a carefree tone. "Really, Steve, you should be ashamed of yourself. Miss Villier doesn't look a bit like a horse, and I'm sure she's much more fun to be with. Besides, if your wife doesn't care, I certainly don't."

"I don't have a wife." Steve's glance caught hers momentarily in the rear-vision mirror. "Neither does Juan."

"Very sensible of you." She turned away to look at the one-story stucco residences scattered around on the hillside. Each unit featured a deep covered porch with gaily striped lounge chairs plus a concrete patio for private sunbathing. "Are these the posh accommodations?" she asked Juan.

He nodded. "Our brochures say 'complete privacy for those who desire it.' We do a big business with the horsy honeymoon set."

Andrea's head came up.

"Two-legged variety, of course," he assured her.

"That's what I hoped you meant." She grasped the door handle as Steve stopped in front of a cottage at the top of the hill. "Is this one mine?"

"All yours," Steve said. "In this location, you'll get all the breeze that's going. There's a nice view over the countryside, too. I imagine the door's unlocked, so if you want to go on in, Juan and I'll bring your things."

"Whatever you say," she agreed stiffly, and moved up the cinder track toward the cottage. As she approached the house, she could hear the whir of the air-conditioning unit mounted on one wall. Two brilliant cardinals were surveying a bird-feeding tray at the far end of the porch from the safety of a nearby bush. Andrea moved softly to avoid startling them, but with her attention diverted, she stumbled as she reached for the door knob. "Darn!" Annoyed, she glanced down to identify the obstruction and then shrank back.

Steve almost ran her down. "Watch it, will you! Don't try to . . . Say, what the devil's the matter?" There was a confused thrash of bodies and bags. Then he successfully

28

clutched her arm after shedding suitcases and the much-maligned coat. "What *is* it?"

"Over there . . . on the floor past the lounge . . . there's a man. . . ."

He was over looking down at the prone figure before she'd finished speaking. With a muttered oath, he squatted on his knees and shook the man by the shoulder . . . hard. "Eric! C'mon—wake up!"

Andrea heard Juan's footsteps on the porch behind her, and then he too had dropped his burdens and was over beside the other two.

"So *this* is where he got to," he said in an undertone which barely reached her ears.

Relieved, now that the victim apparently wasn't a victim at all, Andrea stepped forward to see what was going on. "Who is he?" she asked as Steve administered another shake. "He looks so young. Will he be all right?"

Steve stopped his ministrations long enough to give her a baleful look. "Do you ever stop asking questions?"

"Well, if anybody has a right to—"

"All right, all right." He cut off her expostulation with a brief gesture. "Number one . . . his name is Eric, and he works here on the ranch. Number two, he's eighteen and old enough to know better. Number three, I think so, but I'm not a doctor. We'll move him down to the bunkhouse so he can receive proper attention. Juan . . . give me a hand." He lifted the shoulders of the young ranch hand, whose eyes remained closed as his head sagged forward onto his chest.

"But what's wrong with him? Was he in a fight?" She moved hastily aside as the two men supported the limp figure between them.

Steve moved steadily on with his burden. "I don't think so. He probably managed this all by himself."

She trailed them out to the car and watched them ease Eric's body onto the back seat. Juan got in beside him. "Do you want me to call the office?" she asked plaintively as Steve opened the driver's door.

"All I want you to do"—he punctuated his words by slamming the door in the middle of them and switching on the ignition—"is to go in your cottage and forget you ever saw anything."

"You can't seriously expect me to—"

He cut in ruthlessly, "But if your oversized bump of feminine curiosity won't permit it, at least keep quiet until lunchtime. You'll get all the latest news served with the soup course. If this kind of thing upsets you too much, Miss Sinclair, perhaps you'd be happier away from the Circle C. Give it some thought."

With that he drove off, leaving Andrea in the middle of the road . . . carefully clutching her coat once again.

Chapter TWO

When the big triangle at the corner of the dining hall was rung for lunch, Andrea had at least gotten rid of the miserable coat.

Her "settling in" at the cottage had provided plenty of time for that and unpacking all the other unnecessary items from her suitcases.

Unfortunately she hadn't managed to stow away the memory of that young ranch hand lying so still and helpless on her front porch.

Her mind had sorted out a host of reasons for Eric's collapse while she'd unpacked, showered, and later changed into a sleeveless cotton dress. Then, one by one, she'd discarded her pet theories, knowing that feminine instinct, however appealing, was valueless without a few facts to back it up. All she could do was wait and hope that Eric was well cared for.

In leisurely fashion she had explored her pleasant bed–sitting-room with its stark white walls and color accents of orange and red. A raised modern fireplace, empty now, and a study area with an efficient-looking desk and book-case showed that the ranch owners tried hard to please their guests. But no matter how charming, if the cottage included any more unconscious victims, she'd move to a telephone booth down by the main highway.

Not that she planned to pay any serious attention to Steve's warning; he should have known that his words would make any woman merely dig in her heels. If her determination would help squelch his overbearing ways, so much the better.

The noise of the lunch triangle was a welcome interruption to her thoughts, although it was curiosity rather than hunger which made her so prompt in attending. As she hovered at the dining-room archway a few minutes later to look for a hostess, she was hailed by a voice that could have shattered glass.

"Come in and set. My name's Carter, but you might as well call me 'Grandmaw' . . . everybody else does." A heavyset, gray-haired woman was beckoning commandingly from a big table nearby. She indicated a sulky teenager sitting beside her. "This squirt is my granddaughter Ellie. Don't pay any account to what she says . . . I don't. They tell me your name's Sinclair. Andrea Sinclair. Reckon you don't like folks to call you 'Andy.' "

Andrea smiled and slipped into a chair halfway down the table after consulting a place card above her napkin. "That's right, but I answer to most everything else. Are we the only people eating lunch?"

"They'll straggle in. When you're my age, food's more important than it is when you're younger."

"Then I don't see why you have to drag me in here with you." Her granddaughter spoke up rebelliously, pushing her long black hair back from her forehead. "I'm not a bit hungry."

If she'd only smile, she'd be pretty, Andrea thought. Really pretty. Then she forgot the girl as her glance roamed over the dining hall. The high-ceilinged room was decorated in Spanish style with oak tables and chairs stained almost black. Wine-red was the accent color used in the voluminous floor-to-ceiling draperies lining one wall. At the far end, sliding glass doors opened directly onto the poolside. Andrea's lips pursed in a soundless whistle as she surveyed that spectacular feature. The long, kidney-shaped pool came complete with a waterfall on the side of it. Water splashed down the native stonework while the occasional breeze gently caught the spray and the sunshine made miniature rainbows of the flying drops. Elsewhere, brightly flowered lounges clustered on the concrete apron of the pool under the palm trees and bright green palo verde bushes. The total effect were pure luxury in an oasis type of setting.

"Nice, ain't it?" Grandmaw was watching her shrewdly. "You should see this place in winter. Folks flock here from all over."

"I can imagine." It was difficult for Andrea to bring her attention back to the table.

"There was plenty of time for me to swim a while

longer." Ellie was still complaining. "Why do we have to be first in line to eat? Every day we do the same thing."

"Maybe . . . but it was a waste of time for you to hang around so that you could see Juan," Grandmaw told her. "There was some kind of fuss going on here this morning. Graham lit out for town in the station wagon about an hour ago and took Juan with him."

"Well, you could have told me before," Ellie replied querulously. Then her attention was diverted when a group of men dressed in business suits came through the archway and headed for a long table at the far end of the room. Other than sending one or two bland glances toward the table near the door, the men exhibited none of the curiosity of the casual tourist.

"Trainees." Ellie waved a piece of celery toward the retreating backs. "They're all taking a three-week railroad-management course, so you can cross them off your list. They don't look up except to find another textbook. Absolute total loss." She applied salt to the celery.

"Ellie's right," Grandmaw said. "Those fellows are so busy making a name for themselves that they don't know anybody else is alive. Things are a little slow around here now," she confessed. "Not like some other summers I can remember."

"Then you've been here before?" Andrea probed gently.

"Every year since I sold our spread in Texas. A body gets a hankering to come back to ranch life. Most summers there's a lot goin' on. Last July this place was as busy as a one-eyed cat watching three mouse holes. That's why I brung Ellie this year—I thought she'd like to see a little action."

"And I might as well have stayed home with my ten-year-old brother," the girl broke in. "Juan and Steve are the only two decent men around. . . ."

"Only because that Frenchman . . . Roger . . . doesn't pay any attention to you."

Ellie bestowed a smoldering look on her before continuing, "Juan has to work most of the time, and Steve . . ." She shrugged. "Well, he's busy with the horses."

"Sick ones?" Andrea inquired.

Grandmaw whooped with laughter. "Some horse—that

33

Françoise. Can't blame a man for pickin' a filly like that. Besides, Steve's too old for Ellie."

"Now, that's not very complimentary, Grandmaw. Even if you are right. I was fancying a second childhood." Steve materialized suddenly and tweaked Ellie's hair as he sidled past her to pull out his chair and sit down. "We meet again, Miss Sinclair. Did you enjoy your morning?"

"Loved every minute of it." She lifted her chin defiantly. "I'm sorry now that I didn't plan to stay longer." Her glance played over his freshly ironed denim shirt, noting that his hair was still damp and slicked down from a shower. It must have been a shower, she decided, since Ellie claimed he hadn't been near the pool. "You look more rested, too," she went on. "Did you find time for a nap?"

"Nap? Steve? That's a good one!" Grandmaw slapped the table with the flat of her hand. "Who do you think runs the ranch, girl?"

"You mean Mr. York does it all by himself?" Andrea blinked innocently.

"Hardly." Steve bent over a menu card. "Anything good to eat today?" He obviously chose to change the subject.

Before anyone could reply, Françoise Villier paused in the dining-room archway. She was wearing the same tight jeans belted low on her hips, but she'd changed to a sheer cerise body shirt that must have been attached to her upper half with wallpaper paste. Sometime during her brief stay in America, she'd chosen to follow Women's Lib doctrine and abandon her bra, despite her amply endowed figure. The result was sensational enough to make a cigar-store Indian swivel on his pedestal. As it was, even the railroad men in the corner silenced their conversation reverently as she moved into the room.

"Grapefruit?" Steve said to Andrea.

"I beg your pardon!" Her tone was frigid.

"Why? There's a choice for the first course," he explained blandly. "Broiled grapefruit or iced melon. Oh, Françoise . . . let me help you with that chair." Without giving Andrea another glance, he seated the Frenchwoman on his right.

"*Merci, mon cher.*" She beamed at him before glancing around the table. The Carters were accorded a remote nod in passing, but Andrea received the full battery

34

of attention. "Mees Sinclair, I thought I'd see you at the pool this morning."

"Did you?" Andrea answered warily, still undone by Steve's comment. "I'm sorry. My unpacking took longer than I planned. Perhaps this afternoon."

"This afternoon I can't help you. Roger"—her pronunciation made it come out "Rogair"—"wants me to help him in the shop."

"That's all right. I really hadn't planned on swimming lessons."

Françoise looked down her beautiful nose. "You could use some. I can see your shoulder muscles haven't developed properly."

Andrea's spoon fell from her fingers onto the half-grapefruit which had just been placed in front of her. Carefully she retrieved it as she counted to ten and tried to submerge a sudden savage urge to slam the grapefruit straight across the table. Weak shoulder muscles and all!

Defense came from an unexpected quarter. Steve unfolded his napkin and said, "Lunch isn't the time for a discussion of anthropology, Françoise. It's too hot for serious subjects. Where's your boss today?"

"Around. Roger will be here. I told him about Mees Sinclair, and he likes blondes." She spoke as if Andrea were miles away.

"How kind," Andrea said politely. "And he doesn't mind about the shoulder muscles?"

Françoise shook her head, making her shaggy haircut even shaggier. "No . . . or even about the parka, but he didn't know girls from Iceland entered beauty contests."

At that point Steve choked violently on his iced tea. By the time he'd finished wheezing and having Grandmaw slap his back, the subject had been overshadowed by Roger Villier's arrival.

The man's entrance was almost as theatrical as his cousin's. His clothes were just as bright, and his gaudy body shirt was unbuttoned halfway down his chest, but naturally the results weren't as sensational.

Briskly he pulled out his chair. "'Allo, everybody! I'm sorree to be late. Eef Françoise would help more, I wouldn't 'ave to do all the work by myself. Then I could

35

come to lunch on time." Clearly he wasn't held in thrall by his cousin's vital statistics.

Steve said, "Miss Sinclair, may I present Roger Villier."

"How do you do," Andrea murmured.

"Enchanté." Roger grasped her hand over the top of the table as he bowed deeply. The gesture would have been more effective if he hadn't skimmed a saucer of mayonnaise in the process. "I 'ave heard about *mademoiselle."*

"I hope we can be friends in spite of it," she said.

"Certainement. Be assured of it." He sat down and reached for his wineglass. "Now, what are we eating today?"

There was plenty of time to study him while he was engrossed in the serious business of food. Privately Andrea decided that she could do with less curly brown hair on the chest and a little more on the noggin. Despite that drawback, Roger was a good-looking man of medium height. Almost aggressively so, with brilliant dark eyes, a formidable jawline, and a deep voice full of sensual appeal that could make a woman forget his other failings. From the looks of his deep tan, he evidently spent his spare time on the edge of the swimming pool. She found out shortly that she was wrong about that; he had other loves as well. Four-footed ones.

"You can count on me for the afternoon ride, Steve," he was saying enthusiastically. "Graham said that Eric could watch the shop today, so both Françoise and I can go."

"I'm sorry, Roger." Steve looked up from buttering his roll. "Eric isn't available. He isn't feeling well."

"Maybe he'll feel better later thees afternoon."

"I hope so, but that won't change anything. He isn't even here. . . . Graham took him into town this morning. I thought maybe you knew."

" 'Ow would I know anything? Graham doesn't give me time enough to look outside the door of the shop. Why is eet necessary for Eric to 'ave time off in town today? He doesn't do enough work to get tired." Roger stabbed with his fork for emphasis. "I 'ave told Graham of this, but he says Eric is your responsibility. Now, I am telling you."

"Okay, I've got the message. Would you mind passing the jam."

Roger's scowl deepened. "That's all you intend to do about it? My complaint means nothing?"

Andrea was scarcely conscious of the roast beef being placed in front of her. She wasn't alone in this; all the occupants of her table were avidly following Roger's angry words, and the cooked meat simply wasn't as interesting as the raw meat being served up in front of them.

Steve's lips thinned. "Oh, for God's sake, Roger!" Then, breaking off, as if aware of his audience, he continued more quietly, "Of course I'm interested in hearing your complaints. All of the outside employees are my province . . . you know that. But if you're hoping for a court-martial on the lawn this afternoon, you're out of luck."

"At least you could get this fellow . . . Eric . . . to work for me later," Roger persisted. "Or is that still too much to ask?"

"I'll see if I can find someone."

"What ees the matter with Eric?"

"That's what we're trying to find out." Steve took a bite of his meat and then pushed it aside as if he found it displeasing. He reached out for his glass of iced tea instead. "Graham drove Eric to the hospital in town this morning. The last I heard, he'd been asked to leave him there."

"But there wasn't anything wrong with him last night," Ellie said impulsively.

Steve's glance was sharp. "How do you know? When did you see him?"

"It was after the dance. He asked me to meet him down by the corral." The girl switched to the defensive. "Why? Is there anything wrong with that?"

"Darned right there is!" her grandmother said. "I thought I told you to go to bed after the dance. That's where you said you were going. Maybe I should have checked up on you—the way your mother told me."

Ellie's face crumpled. "This is the first time I've sneaked out, Grandmaw, and there wasn't anything wrong with it. Eric just wanted to see me alone for a while. What's so bad about that?" She raised her head to survey them all

37

angrily. "If you're my age, you can't do anything, but it's all right to hang around a man when you're older. Isn't it, Françoise?"

"Stop it, Ellie," Steve cut in.

"Go to your room, girl." Grandmaw's voice overrode him. "You can apologize to Françoise later."

"I don't see why I have to." The teen-ager shoved back her chair and got to her feet. "Nobody likes to hear the truth. That's what Eric said just last night, and he was right."

"Your room, I said." There was steel in the older woman's tone.

"All right . . . I'm going. I wouldn't stay here now if you begged me to!" Ellie flounced toward the end of the room and disappeared without looking back.

"I'm sorry, Françoise," Grandmaw mumbled with embarrassment. "The girl hasn't learned to watch her tongue."

"Pooh! Who cares what a girl that age says? She's 'aving trouble with 'er glands." Françoise reached over and calmly took an apricot from the platter of fresh fruit.

Grandmaw's attention was distracted momentarily by the plateful of food placed in front of her. She scowled at it, and then at the waitress. "This isn't what I ordered."

"It *is* what you ordered, Mrs. Carter." The girl was firm.

"I ordered roast beef, rare."

"That *is* roast beef, rare."

"Where?"

"There!" The waitress pushed the plate more firmly in front of the older woman.

"Humph! Looks done to a cinder to me. Oh, all right." Grandmaw picked up her fork and turned back to Françoise. "There's absolutely nothing wrong with my granddaughter's hormones."

"I 'ave said 'glands.' You didn't hear right."

"So now I'm deaf!" The fork was banged down on the table. "Let me tell you, young lady—there's nothing wrong with my ears. You sat there and implied that Ellie was light-headed in her attic. I won't stand for that kind of talk."

"Ladies . . . ladies . . . another time, *s'il vous plaît*." Roger held his head theatrically. "Madame Carter, I beg of you—pay no attention to my cousin. I am sorry that my uncle sent 'er to me to learn English."

"I'm not." Françoise spit her apricot pit into a saucer with evident enjoyment.

Steve turned to Andrea and said in an undertone, "At this rate, we'll have to refund your money. I apologize . . . most of the time we display better manners. It must be the humidity or something today."

She frowned at him. "Don't you have your scripts mixed? This morning you were suggesting that I go home. After Eric . . . remember?"

"Now, that was a mistake—it was the wrong approach with a woman. For a while there, I forgot."

"That's your trouble."

"I don't follow you."

"Maybe you've been around horses too long." She blotted her lips with a napkin. "We have a different set of rules."

"It's possible." His thick sun-bleached eyebrows drew together. "Well, if you don't respond to commands—how about a little persuasion?"

"That wasn't what I meant."

"No? Let's see what happens." He took a lump from the sugar bowl and gravely offered it to her. "From me to you, Miss Sinclair."

Confused, she pulled back.

"Are you showing Andrea how to make friends with her horse, Steve?" Grandmaw had simmered down and was watching from her end of the table. "Don't let him frighten you, Andrea. He'll make sure you get a nice calm one. Graham doesn't want his paying guests going home in a sling."

"Some women need all the help they can get." Françoise was searching for another ripe apricot. "Graham *did* say you rode, didn't he?"

Andrea mumbled something in her cup of coffee. By then, confessing that she didn't ride would have been like admitting she couldn't count past ten with her shoes on.

Steve was watching her closely. "Maybe you'd better come out a little early, and I'll get you fixed up. Don't forget to wear pants and a long-sleeved shirt."

"In this heat?" She was aghast.

"Take another look at those cactus if you have any doubts. You'd come back in ribbons otherwise."

Andrea took a second swallow of coffee and manfully refrained from stating that it was a distinct possibility anyway.

By four o'clock, her inward feelings hadn't changed; her stomach muscles were still tied in a bow knot at the idea of clambering on a horse. Outwardly, it was a different story. Her new outfit included beige wool gabardine slacks, brown jodhpur boots, and a long-sleeved denim blouse that might have been comfortable for the Rockies in December. In an Arizona summer, she felt as if she should be making for the nearest mental hospital rather than the corral.

Steve chose to ignore her flaming cheeks as she came up the stable path. He straightened from his relaxed position against the fence and ground out his cigarette with the heel of his boot. "For lord's sake, don't you have a hat?" was his only comment.

"No." She drew up beside him. "Only coats. At least I managed to find some slacks. . . ."

"Jeans would be cooler." He was surveying her dubiously.

"I'll go into town tomorrow and buy a pair. Right now this is the best I can do."

He rubbed the side of his nose. "Sorry. I guess it didn't occur to me that some people aren't fitted for horses."

"In more ways than one. . . ."

"I beg your pardon?"

"Never mind." She moved through a wide doorway toward the tackroom, where she heard the whir of an airconditioner. "Why don't I wait here until the others come?"

"Don't you even want to see the horse you'll be riding?" He had paused beside a long shelf where saddles were stored. Individual horses' names were marked under each one.

She smiled reluctantly. "I didn't know we had to be formally introduced. What's the name of my gallant steed?" Curious now, she peered at the place on the shelf from which he had taken a worn Western saddle. "Hammerhead?" Her voice rose. "He sounds like a Dick Tracy character! Are you *sure* he's gentle?"

40

"Of course he is."

"I think I'll take a look, after all." Grimly she followed him to the back of the tackroom, where a wide Dutch door opened into the corral. Peering over the lower part, she noticed five saddled horses standing in the dusty stableyard. "Which one?"

Steve opened the bottom part of the door and went out, closing it carefully behind him. "I haven't saddled yours yet. He's down there." He nodded toward the bottom of the corral, where another dozen horses were standing patiently beside wooden feed racks and a concrete watering trough. All horses except one.

He was lying sprawled on his side in the sunshine, very much like a town drunk who had passed out after a night at the corner saloon. Occasionally his long tail would swish and bring up a scattering of dust, which settled unevenly over his white coat.

Andrea raised a stricken face. "Hammerhead?"

"Hammerhead," Steve concurred. "Now, wait a minute . . ." He caught her elbow as she would have turned away. "You'll have to take my word for it. He's the gentlest one in the stable."

"I can see that. Does he ever get vertical, or do I try side-saddle?"

"He'll get up . . . fast . . . when he sees me coming with a saddle. Why, he practically looks like a blood brother to that horse of the Lone Ranger's when he has some trappings on! You just go back in and relax by the air-conditioner." He nudged her away from the door.

She darted another despairing look toward the bottom of the corral. "Could you manage to dust him off a little when you saddle him?"

"I'll blow hard," he promised, grinning. The tired lines that she'd noticed in his face earlier in the day seemed to have disappeared. "Go sit down . . . I won't be long."

"That's what I'm afraid of," she murmured to herself as she watched him stride easily down through the corral. She turned away before he reached the mottled white form reclining beyond the trough. There was no point in facing Hammerhead any sooner than she had to.

"Hi, Andrea! How are you settling in?" Juan came in the other door of the tackroom. "Have you gotten used to our temperature yet?"

"I've learned to move from air-conditioner to ice cubes to the bathtub, so far," she admitted as she went over and sat down in a rawhide chair. "In another day, I'll say 'What temperature?'"

"That's the girl." He inserted a coin in the canned-pop machine beside him and waited for the soft drink to fall. "Will you have something?"

"No, thank you." She crossed her knees and surveyed her polished jodhpur boots ruefully. "When I come back from this ride, I think I'll need something stronger than ginger ale."

"So that's what you're waiting for." He moved over to the Dutch door and looked out into the corral. "Hammerhead, eh? Well"—he shrugged and took a swallow of his cold drink—"Steve knows what he's doing."

"Ummm . . . I hope so. Are you coming along on this junket?"

"It depends whether they need me. If I go, I'll be just that much later getting my work done. There've been too many interruptions already."

Andrea waited hopefully for him to expand about Eric and the sudden trip to town, but he changed the subject.

"Graham realizes that I should be spraying the horses instead of riding them. The flies are mighty thick for this early in the season."

She got up and went over beside him to stare out at the saddled horses in the corral. "That's a pretty slick arrangement when they're standing around," she commented. "Your neighbor brushes the flies from your face with his tail, and you do the same for him. What do you call it—heel and toe?"

"That's plain horse sense." Juan deposited his empty pop can in a wastebasket and grinned at her. "I keep forgetting this life is all new to you."

"And you're an old hand at the game." She smiled in response and went over to a nearby hatrack. "Would anybody mind if I borrowed one of these brimmed hats?"

"Help yourself. That's what they're there for. Here—let me help you." He came over beside her. "This one should fit. No, don't tilt it—wear it straight on your head. Hey, that looks good."

"I'm catching on," she said, pleased. "You must get tired of taking care of greenhorns."

He shoved his hands in his back pockets. "I haven't been here long enough to get tired of the guests. It looks like a pretty good life to me."

"I thought you were one of the founding fathers."

"Nope, I'm almost as new as you. Steve phoned and asked me to come to work here about three weeks ago . . . right after he came. Graham had told him to go ahead and hire more help."

"You mean Steve is new here, too?" She stared at him.

"Sure. Is that bad? A man can learn to handle live-stock in lots of places, you know."

Andrea went slowly back to her chair and lowered herself on the arm of it. "Is the whole staff new at Circle C?"

He scratched his jaw. "Graham's been here for several years, but Françoise came just a little before Steve. That was right after the owner decided to enlarge the gift shop and sweeten the profits."

"But the other ranch hands . . . ?"

Carelessly, "You'll have to ask Steve." Juan glanced toward the corral. "He's on his way now with your faithful steed. Damn!" The exclamation came out softly.

"Now what?"

"He's collected Ellie, too. That girl hangs on the fence waiting for the rides to begin."

"From the conversation at lunch, that isn't the only reason she hangs around." Andrea told him dryly. "She was also holding down the edge of the swimming pool this morning, and I gathered she wasn't waiting for Françoise."

A dull red crept up Juan's neck. "That's one of the harder parts of this job. Ellie's at the age to be so damned . . . intense . . . about things. How do you tell a girl to take it easy?"

"Heavens . . . don't ask me." Andrea held up her hands defensively. "Let her down easy, though. The poor girl's had enough trouble today."

"What do you mean?"

"Since you've proved elusive, she's apparently discovered Eric. She took it hard when she heard that young man was in the hospital."

Juan muttered something unprintable and shoved his hands deeper in his pockets.

Andrea frowned at him. "What's wrong with that? Honestly, you're as bad as her grandmother. An eighteen-year-old girl can't be blamed for wanting some masculine attention, and Eric is a good-looking young man. . . ."

"You sound like a high-school guidance counselor, and I've never seen anybody who looked less like one." He jerked his head toward the open door. "C'mon over here and take a look at your transportation."

Andrea got up reluctantly. "All right, if you say so," she replied, going over to stand beside him. An inner part of her mind noted that Mr. Núñez was as closemouthed as Steve when it came to skirting answers and changing the subject. She couldn't blame them for not wanting to dwell on Eric's failings, but it seemed strange to dismiss him so completely.

"Hi there, Juan!" Ellie was a different person as she greeted him enthusiastically. "Steve said you'd be here and take us out for the ride today."

"Oh?" Juan looked disconcerted, but he managed a weak grin. "Well, if that's the plan . . ."

"It is." Steve came up to the doorway behind them. "You and Ellie can take the string up to the office. Her grandmother and the Villiers will meet you there."

"What about Andrea?" Juan asked, still confused. "I thought she was going with us."

"Things have changed." Steve shoved his hat slightly up on his forehead, leaving a mark on the tanned skin. He looked hot, and his next words showed it. "Let's get going, shall we? Take the rim trail . . . I'll see you later."

"But, Steve . . ." Ellie's puzzled face showed she was just catching on. "You mean you're going out, too? Why aren't you coming with us? I've never known you to give private rides before." Her brooding gaze swung to Andrea. "Why does Miss Sinclair rate special attention?"

"Honestly, I don't know what this is all about," Andrea started to say, before Steve cut her off brusquely.

"Don't be silly, chicken." He reached over and ruffled Ellie's thick hair. "You and Juan will be leading the fast ride today—these horses need some real exercise. Since I have to inspect the fence near the gully, I thought I'd check out Miss Sinclair at the same time. She needs it before she goes with a more advanced group."

44

Andrea's eyes flashed. "I'm still here, you know," she began, only to have Juan give her a warning glance.

"Steve's right," he said, settling his hat and taking Ellie's elbow. "We'll be on our way, or Françoise will come down here raising cain. C'mon, Ellie." He swung up on a glossy bay after knotting the reins of two other saddled horses. "Get on that nag of yours and lead Jolly for your grandmother."

"Don't call my darling Gypsy a nag," the girl protested, following him happily into the corral and patting a spirited pinto before she, too, went easily up into the saddle. "I'll race you to the drive. . . ."

"Come back here, *chiquita!* You know better than that. . . ." Juan's voice trailed off as they departed in a cloud of corral dust.

Andrea turned to Steve with a hard-to-read expression on her face. "Should I apologize for taking you away from your ride?"

He snorted. "Hardly. There was no point in letting you in for a bunch of static from Ellie and Françoise. Women can be the very devil." Shaking his head, he pulled his hat back down over his eyes. "Let's go. If I leave Hammerhead alone much longer, he'll be lying down again."

"Do you think I need a horse *that* calm?" She trailed him out into the sunshine. "Even Shetland ponies stand up once in a while." Her sentence ended abruptly as she saw the white horse tethered to the fence rail. "My lord, he's so tall!"

"Well, he won't shrink to size." Steve sounded as if he were thoroughly tired of feminine vagaries. "Most beginners don't complain about the way a poor horse looks."

"I don't mean to be difficult." She was still staring at the rawboned creature in front of her. "But he's big enough to be a steeplechaser."

"Not Hammerhead. He wouldn't open his eyes wide enough to see a jump six inches away." Steve was untying the reins. "He's only interested in one thing. . . ."

"Biting the hand that feeds him?" She was clutching a sugar cube in her palm.

"Certainly not." Steve slapped the white horse carelessly on the neck. That was a mistake, as a cloud of dust immediately filled the air. "Sorry."

Andrea noticed that he was trying to keep a straight

45

face and not doing well. "Never mind," she said, resigned. "Here, Hammerhead . . ." She offered the sugar cube on her open palm, bending her fingers back as far as possible when the long dusty nose came around snuffling. The sugar was promptly inhaled through soft lips, while a pair of rheumy blue eyes surveyed her with newfound interest. "Hey . . . that's all I have," she protested as he nuzzled closer.

Steve pulled him back by the bridle. "Okay, that takes care of the amenities. Sooner or later you'll have to get on top of him. Come over to this side."

She skirted around Hammerhead's not inconsiderable derriere and stood beside Steve.

He bent forward. "I'll give you a leg up."

Before she had time to think, he had pitched her neatly into the saddle.

"Hang on to the reins . . . not the horn," he instructed tersely. "That's the way. Now, grip with your knees. Don't look so scared; he isn't going anywhere yet."

"I wish you'd tell *him* . . . not me." Andrea took one look down past her stirrup and then hastily raised her glance. It was like peering off a two-story building. Her fingers tightened on the reins, and Hammerhead turned his head speculatively. "Whoa, there . . . nice boy," she crooned, so that he couldn't conceivably think he was being directed to leave. When Steve came back from a corner of the stable leading a well-mannered chestnut, she asked, "Is there anything I should know about him? Like bad habits . . ."

Steve swung up into his saddle. "Just one. He's prone to chase dead rattlesnakes."

"Oh, that could be dangerous." Then, as his words sank in, "Very funny, Mr. York."

He chuckled as he brought his horse alongside. "It's a very old joke, Miss Sinclair. Come on . . . I'll lead the way. We'll take it nice and easy—single file on the path beyond the fence. Let Hammerhead do the work. You just sit there and get the feel of things. Keep him moving, though."

"If you say so." She flicked the reins gingerly. "Okay Hammerhead—Geronimo!"

Steve sent her a quizzical glance. "That's what the parachutists say."

"I know. I'm prepared for the worst."

The two horses set off at a sedate walk. Within the first ten minutes, Andrea discovered that keeping Hammerhead moving was a full-time job. His idea of motion consisted solely of drifting from one edible plant to the next. He would snatch a bite on the move occasionally, but most of the time it involved considerable effort to get his head out of the nearest bit of vegetation. Cactus, mesquite, or palo verde—it was all one to the rawboned white horse. One long continuous snack.

"For God's sake, keep his head up," Steve said finally when he looked back for the third time and discovered Hammerhead stalled again. "Kick him in the ribs."

Andrea raised shocked eyes. "I couldn't. Don't you ever feed this poor animal?"

"Not until the end of the day, or we couldn't get him out of the corral."

She shook her head stubbornly. "I can't hurt him."

"The only way you could do that would be by putting him on a diet. Make him move." He watched her with exasperation. "Don't just pat him—show him who's boss."

"He already knows."

"Maybe Françoise was right about those underdeveloped shoulder muscles of yours," he taunted.

That did it. Andrea's hand came down on Hammerhead's rump in a swat that made the horse move forward in sheer surprise. "Good boy!" she praised, and moved her operation forward to pat him appreciatively on the neck. A second dust cloud swirled up into her face.

"Keep him moving on that short rein," Steve instructed, paying no attention to her discomfort. "Let's increase the pace a little. Hang on! You'll be all right." He dug his heels into his horse's flanks, and the chestnut moved into a gentle trot. Hammerhead grudgingly followed in his tracks.

The ride went on and on. By the time another quarter-hour had passed, Andrea's legs ached and her wrists were numb with the death grip on the reins. After a half-hour, the surrounding saguaro cactus and sunbaked earth fused into an unidentifiable mass in her mind. She was only conscious of the hot still air and molten sun above. Gritting her teeth, she forced herself to stay upright in the saddle and concentrate on Hammerhead's turned-back ears. Clearly he was unhappy, too.

Ahead of her, Steve rode like a robot, merely glancing back occasionally to see that she was still vertical. Evidently the temperature had no effect on him; his stance didn't alter, and his body remained a relaxed appendage above the graceful-moving chestnut.

Andrea could feel the perspiration drip down her back and between her breasts. If she ever got back to the ranch, she decided hazily, they wouldn't be able to pry her away from the air-conditioner.

Steve finally pulled up at a fork in the path. "This is a shortcut," he said, indicating a twisting trail to the left. "I think we'd better take it. You've probably had enough for the first day."

"Whatever you say." Her voice sounded thin to her own ears.

"Then we'll bear left," he said tersely, urging his horse forward.

Hammerhead's ears flickered with interest, and he picked up his tempo voluntarily. Andrea swayed and clutched the saddlehorn with both hands.

When they reached the south end of the corral, the path descended sharply into a dry riverbed. Andrea was taken unawares by Hammerhead's vertical plunge down the bank and felt her feet slipping from the stirrups. She fell forward, half out of the saddle, her nose buried in a coarse mane and her arms embracing—embracing, for heaven's sake!—Hammerhead's dirty neck.

His rider's predicament didn't faze her zealous steed. Only one thing was paramount in his mind just then— he was nearly home at last! The final twenty yards were done in a burst of speed that made Steve's mount skitter sideways as the big white horse went by.

"Whoa, there! Pull him in!" Steve was on the ground by her side in an instant. Just in time to clutch Hammerhead's bridle with one hand and catch Andrea's falling figure with the other.

Her legs folded when they hit the ground, and she would have sunk right on down if he hadn't gripped her in a way that made her ribs ache. The only part of her body that wasn't aching already, she thought despairingly.

"Andrea . . . are you all right?" Strangely, his voice was miles away. Then the afternoon sun disappeared in a mist, and she simply sagged in his arms.

Chapter THREE

The next thing Andrea knew, she was being tucked in the front seat of the station wagon parked by the corral. Her door was closed carefully before Steve moved around to the driver's side and started the car.

She struggled to sit upright. "Really, you don't have to do this. I can manage perfectly well if you'll just give me a minute."

"Sit quietly," he cut her off emphatically. "I'll have you up to your cottage in no time at all." Then, as the car churned up the roadway, "Why didn't you say something, you crazy galoot?"

She shook her head, but the panic that had come over her melted away at his protective tone. "I didn't know— honestly. It was terribly hot, and then, when I finally reached the corral, everything became one big blur." She sighed softly. "I think Hammerhead beat you out at the wire. It was close enough for a photo finish, wasn't it?"

"That damned horse!"

"It wasn't his fault." Her dizziness was receding, but she kept her head braced against the seat and the side of the car. "Don't you have to rub him down or something?"

"At the moment, your rubdown comes first."

Her flushed cheeks took on additional color as she turned her head and stared at his profile. Surely he didn't think she would allow anything of the sort. "That won't be necessary," she managed as he pulled up in the front of her cottage. "Thank you very much for bringing me, but I won't need any more help. . . ." The words petered out when she saw that he was ignoring her completely.

Instead he got out, walked around the car, and yanked open her door. "This way," he commanded, leaning forward.

"You needn't bother, I tell you. Oh, for heaven's sake—I can certainly walk. If you'll just put me down . . ."

"I could do with less advice and more cooperation at this point," he said pointedly as he pulled up at her screen door. "Is this locked?"

From the vicinity of his shoulder, she shook her head. It was difficult to remain aloof in his arms, when the natural reaction was to let her body relax against the firm strength of his.

"Good." Somehow he got a hand free to turn the knob and shoved the door open with a force that sent it flying back against the wall. As he carried her inside, the cooled air felt like pure balm after the soaring temperatures on the ride. Gently he lowered her to the bed and went back to close the door.

She pushed herself up on her elbows. "Thanks very much. I can manage now. Steve—will you listen to me! I can certainly take off my own boots."

"Look, for the last time, just lie there and keep quiet." Although he didn't raise his voice, there was a snap to his words that made her instantly sink back against the pillows. "The first thing to do is get you out of these clothes. Tomorrow, for God's sake, go into town and buy something to wear that wouldn't double for the Arctic Circle." He tossed her second boot into the corner after the first before moving up to the waistband zipper on her slacks. By that time, Andrea was too weary to struggle. She even cooperated by lifting her hips so the gabardine slacks could be pulled off easily. "Where's your robe?" he asked, straightening by the side of the bed. "I presume you have something that isn't wool or flannel?"

She nodded toward the dressing room. "In there . . . hanging in the closet." The cool air felt marvelous on her skin, and she could feel her tense muscles relaxing. After all, she told herself, people wore less than she had on at the swimming pool. Naturally, the undressing process wasn't going any further.

She was wrong. Steve came back carrying a soft green nylon peignoir, which he tossed on the bed. Then he reached over to strip off her long-sleeved shirt with the deft impersonality he would have used to peel an artichoke.

"Don't go into shock," he said then, with the first touch of dry amusement. "That's as far as we go."

"I should hope so." Andrea was intensely conscious of her bare shoulders above a lacy white bra. She sat up to help him put the robe around her.

"Now, lie back. Close your eyes and take it easy while I get some stuff from the car. How's the dizziness, by the way?" he asked.

"Much better."

"Any nausea?"

"It's almost gone, thank heavens."

"Good. Sounds as if you got off fairly easy." He pushed her gently back on the pillow and got up, to disappear through the front door. He was back almost immediately, carrying a metal first-aid box. The next thing Andrea knew, a thermometer was being thrust between her lips.

"No editorial comment," Steve said, forestalling her automatic protest.

She watched him move over to the tiny refrigerator in the corner of the room and extract an ice-cube tray, taking it with him as he disappeared into the bathroom. It wasn't long until he came back with a black-and-white-striped ice bag balanced on his palm. This was deposited firmly on her forehead.

Andrea's reaction would have been more forceful if it hadn't felt so wonderful.

By then, he had extracted the thermometer and read it, before grinning down at her. "You'll live to ride another day, Miss Sinclair," he said in a solemn tone.

She matched it faithfully. "That's a relief. Cancel the call to my lawyer. I'll put off suing you until tomorrow." Pushing the ice bag to a more rakish angle, she added, "Thank you for your help. I really feel much better."

"Good. See that you continue the treatment." He moved away from the bedside to perch on the arm of a chair. "Incidentally, that ice bag is part of the prescription. Keep it on for another hour or so. In the meantime, I'll send up one of the waitresses with some tea." He frowned slightly. "It would probably be better if you had room service for dinner. You should stay where it's cool for the rest of the day."

"If you think it's necessary."

"Advisable, at least. I'm sorry this happened—it was my

51

fault. My only excuse was that I had other things on my mind, and I didn't realize you were feeling the heat."

"It crept up on me, too," Andrea confessed. "I guess I was overtired to start with. Probably I would have said something, only . . ." Her voice faltered.

"You were too damned stubborn to give in," he finished grimly.

She moved restlessly on the pillow. "Let's forget the whole thing, shall we?"

His expression lightened. "Maybe that's best. Will you be all right now if you're left alone? I should get back down and take care of those horses."

"Of course. I hope they're all right."

"The worst that could happen is that Hammerhead has started gnawing on the corral fence because he thinks he's missed dinner. It's a daily complaint with him." Steve paused by the door. "I'll send a girl up with the hot tea for you. In the meantime . . ."

"I know. Stay here and be quiet."

"Exactly. I wouldn't mind a prescription like that myself." He was out of the door before Andrea could figure out exactly what he meant.

The rest of the afternoon and early evening passed uneventfully. Tea was brought by a solicitous waitress, and shortly afterward a pleasant middle-aged woman who announced herself as the Circle C's housekeeper knocked on the door.

"Mr. York asked me to stop by and check your temperature, Miss Sinclair," she said politely when Andrea called for her to come in.

"Thank you, but there's no need for all this bother. I feel like an awful fraud."

"You shouldn't. It's a pity this happened. Sunstroke can be very uncomfortable." The woman was shaking down a thermometer as she spoke. "Mr. Brinkley will call the doctor if this isn't normal." She popped it in Andrea's mouth and smiled. "I'll get some more ice for that bag of yours while we're waiting. You just lie still."

There was a positive conspiracy to keep her off her feet, Andrea decided with resignation, and sank back on her pillows.

When the housekeeper removed the thermometer a few minutes later, her pleased expression announced the results. "Everything's normal, Miss Sinclair. You must have a strong constitution." She put the thermometer in its case and bent over to straighten the bedspread. "Mr. York thought you'd prefer dinner here rather than going down for it. How does roast lamb sound to you?"

"Fine, thanks." Andrea balanced the ice bag obediently on her head, but she pushed up to a sitting position. "After dinner, though, I insist on reverting to normal. All this coddling will have a bad effect on me."

"After you've eaten, I promise that we'll leave you alone. One of the girls will bring your dinner tray in about half an hour." The housekeeper went to the window and rearranged the edge of the curtain. "From the looks of the clouds over the mountains, we might be having a little rain later tonight."

"Is that bad?"

The other shook her head. "The cooler air would be a relief. I was just thinking of the dance. We hold it out on the court by the swimming pool, and if it rains, we'll have to cancel it."

"Are there enough people here for a dance?"

"Oh my, yes! Everybody joins in. The staff enjoys them as much as the guests. You should walk down after dark and listen to the music, even if you don't feel like dancing, Miss Sinclair."

"Thanks, I'll see how energetic I am by then."

"That's a good idea." The woman opened the door and nodded affably. "I'll tell Mr. Brinkley that you're on the mend, but be sure and take more care on your ride tomorrow. We don't like to have our guests under the weather. Good night for now."

"Good night . . . and thank you again."

When the door had closed behind her, Andrea stared thoughtfully at the wall opposite her bed. The muted roar of the air-conditioner barely disturbed the quiet of the cottage, and already she had learned to tune it out. Her glance flicked over a raised-hearth fireplace which loomed emptily in the middle of the whitewashed wall. A rectangular plaque in intricately carved silver rested on the shallow fireplace mantel. Part of Andrea's mind noted the laborious workmanship of a bird design, while the rest of her thoughts were still concerned with the housekeeper's words about the evening's entertainment.

Evidently the ranch dances made it easy for guests and staff to meet each other, so that impressionable girls like Ellie could further an acquaintance with young men like Eric. At least Grandmaw Carter wouldn't have to worry tonight, with Eric in a Tucson hospital. Probably Juan Núñez would be around to help fill the gap. Andrea thoughtfully shoved the ice bag down against her hot cheek. If Juan attended the dances, chances were that Steve did, too. Françoise would see to that. Andrea's mouth suddenly became a straight line of displeasure. The Frenchwoman was a pure pain in the neck—a decided liability with feminine guests. Perhaps Graham felt she was such a hit with the masculine ones that it shifted the balance in her favor.

Andrea's spirits rose when her dinner tray arrived. By the time she'd finished eating, however, her solitary confinement in the cottage was beginning to pall. She went over to turn on the television, but it was more insipid than usual, with reruns on every channel. Discouraged, she pushed the "off" button and moved restlessly around the room. So far her holiday wasn't exactly a rousing success; her first night at the Circle C, and the major entertainment was watching three moths circle the light bulb.

Irritably she turned off the offending overhead fixture and slipped out onto the darkened front porch of the cottage. It wouldn't hurt to get some fresh air and see if the dance was worth attending. A persistent inner voice told her to stop fooling herself: all she wanted to know was whether Steve York was at the dance—alone.

Standing well back in the shadows, Andrea discovered that her viewpoint was excellent. Below her, the waxed dance floor by the pool was clearly illuminated by colored spotlights, and music from the powerful amplifier floated upward on the soft night air.

The city lights of Tucson made a colorful display far to the west, but in other directions the uninhabited parkland looked black and forbidding. In fact, the only nearby evidence of civilization seemed to be the tiny lights illuminating the cottage paths on the hillside around her.

She gave an involuntary shiver. The dance music below was a welcome relief from the solitude and immensity of the surrounding desert. It would have been more com-

forting if some of the other cottages were occupied—
rather than having the entire hillside to herself. No wonder
Eric had been able to escape detection on her front
porch!

At that thought, she gave herself a mental shake to
change the subject. There was no point in adding a nervous breakdown to a simple case of sunstroke. Either she
should get dressed and go down to the dance or go back
inside and settle for a poor movie on television. Her hand
was on the doorknob when the sound of voices made her
pause and look back over her shoulder.

A couple had wandered away from the dance and were
strolling along the path leading to the office.

"Ellie, I wish you'd get hold of yourself. . . ." It was
Juan's voice, Andrea decided, and she moved instinctively
back into deeper shadows by the door. His tone showed
that the two of them hadn't chosen the deserted path for
romantic reasons.

"Oh, it's easy for you to say," the girl responded resent-
fully. "You never liked him. Eric never had a chance
with any of you . . . even Steve wouldn't give him a
break." She pulled her arm from his clasp.

"If you listened to that muck, you *were* a little fool."
He hauled her back beside him on the path. "It's no wonder your grandmother's keeping you on a short rein. Remember, *chica*, I'm responsible for you tonight. . . . Do
any more fiddling around, and you'll be yanked home."

"Since when is making a telephone call 'fiddling
around'?" Ellie's voice rose. "It's still a free country, and
I had every right to call Eric in the hospital."

"And a lot of good it did you. All you found out was
that your friend Eric had disappeared. That's how much
he cared for you or anybody else. The hospital was his
one last chance for help, and he turned it down."

Andrea frowned as she heard the new development.
Why in the world would Eric sign himself out of the
hospital without permission?

Ellie answered her unspoken question, the words coming distinctly across the quiet night air. "He felt everyone was against him, anyhow—he didn't have a chance."
She tossed her head and added proudly, "Eric can take
care of himself . . . you'll see."

"Only a fool would go along with that kind of thinking. Your grandmother's right—you'd better go home and grow up." Juan quickened his pace, and the two of them passed by Andrea's cottage without giving it a glance.

His sharp words evidently had some effect. For the first time Ellie's voice wavered. "I don't want to go home, Juan. At least you listen to me . . . sometimes."

"When you get over your adolescent crushes, I'll be more impressed."

She was still resentful. "Eric didn't treat me like a baby. He gave me credit for having some sense—which is more than you do."

"Well, stay away from him from now on. Otherwise you're asking for trouble, *chica*." His voice lightened as he put his arm around her shoulders. "C'mon, I'll buy you a Coke, and we can both cool off. Okay?"

"Oh, yes!" Her silhouette moved close against his side as they reached the corner of the building. "Then we can still go back to the dance. It's early yet."

Andrea grimaced as their voices faded. Thank goodness she hadn't been caught in her eavesdropping role. Her glance went back to the scene below as the dance music resumed. This time she easily identified Steve York's tall figure strolling across the lighted surface of the dancing space. He didn't pause to talk with any of the couples around him, but moved purposefully toward the path that led up to her cottage.

The simple happening made her suddenly feel as young as Ellie, and her heart rate picked up enthusiastically. If the man was actually going to come and see her, he might suggest going to the dance. It wouldn't do to appear too eager, she decided, but it certainly wouldn't hurt to go back in the cottage and put on some lipstick . . . just in case.

She glanced over her shoulder for a last reassuring look before she went through the doorway, and then froze in consternation. Steve had paused on the path in response to a hail from Françoise, who was by the poolside.

As Andrea watched, the Frenchwoman, clad in a flowing evening skirt and clinging top, hurried up the path to Steve's side. She greeted him with some laughing remark and threaded her arm possessively through his. He resisted for a moment, arguing with her, before bending down to salute her upturned lips. The kiss didn't last long, but it wasn't a halfhearted effort on either side. Since Andrea had nothing to do but study it in detail, she was well qualified to give an opinion. Numbly she watched the two of them finally turn back to the dance—arm-in-arm. The echo of Françoise's laughter still hung in the air as Andrea went in the cottage and closed the door firmly behind her.

The telephone began to ring as she turned on the light by her bed. Slowly she bent over and lifted the receiver. "Yes?"

"Miss Sinclair?" The manager's hearty voice sounded less hearty after her curt monosyllable. "This is Graham Brinkley. I understand you're feeling better after your little upset."

"I'm fine, thank you."

He was still puzzled at her formality. "I'm delighted to hear it. Frankly, I expected Steve to show more perception . . ."

Andrea's face was bleak. So did I, she thought, so did I.

". . . but since it's all history now, I hoped you'd come down to the dance tonight as my partner," Graham was saying. "We need all the beautiful women we can get, and I know you'd enjoy meeting our other new guests."

"I'm sure I would, Mr. Brinkley"—she tried to infuse some warmth in her tone—"but I'm really too tired tonight. Let's make it another time."

"Of course—if you honestly mean it."

Andrea felt a twinge of conscience at his obvious disappointment. Not enough, however, to spend the night watching Françoise flaunt her conquest around a dance floor.

"I do," she assured Graham. "Perhaps you'd show me your collection of Indian art tomorrow if there's a spare minute."

"I'll do more than that—I'll take you to the museum in town so you can see some really choice pieces." Enthusiasm was back in his voice. "Afterwards, we'll visit the Desert Museum to give you the real feeling for our life in the Southwest."

"That sounds very nice," Andrea said, knowing she should be grateful and wishing she could howl instead.

It wasn't Graham's fault that the itinerary sounded as if it should be taken for college credit.

"We'll plan lunch in town," he was saying. "It will do me good to get away from the ranch for a while. Françoise can take care of the office; if she has any problems, she can always call on Steve."

"That's convenient," Andrea murmured.

"So let's figure on leaving about ten in the morning. Is that all right with you?"

"Fine. I'll look forward to it."

"So will I," he confessed boyishly. "Now—you're sure there's nothing else I can do tonight?"

"Not a thing." She forced a cheerful note into her voice. "See you in the morning."

"Right. Good night, then, Andrea."

His receiver went down, and she replaced hers automatically. As she turned back the sheet on her bed, she went over the conversation in her mind. Graham's last offer made her smile despite herself. There certainly wasn't anything that he or anybody else could do to salvage this day! It had been a disaster from the time she woke up until the romantic byplay a few minutes ago.

She sighed as she sat down wearily on the edge of the bed. The only thing needed to really put a finishing touch on it was to find a black-widow spider under her pillow. She smiled again, wryly. Given a few more hours, Françoise could probably have managed even that.

Chapter FOUR

By morning Andrea had recovered her sense of humor along with a sense of well-being brought on by the sunshine and the clear, smogless sky.

Françoise was accorded only a single fleeting thought, and Steve was dismissed with a tolerant shrug. If Mr. York preferred clinging brunettes, so be it. In the meantime, she could look forward to her day with Graham and consign last night's worries to the wastebasket.

She phoned for room service, and after finishing a continental breakfast, dressed carefully in a sleeveless orange linen. The final touch to her outfit was a matching Italian straw hat with a floppy brim. Today she was taking no more chances with the powerful desert sun!

On the walk down to the office, she stopped occasionally to watch the flocks of birds that twittered in the palo verde and prickly ocotillo bushes. The bright red cardinals were a constant splash of color against the muted desert background, while the cactus wrens and doves blended easily with the natural camouflage. They flitted to the scattered bird-feeding platforms like suburban commuters heading for the station. Overhead the sun beat steadily down.

Andrea found Graham in the cool recesses of the office with the telephone receiver to his ear.

He grinned at her, and cupping his hand over the mouthpiece, said, "Go on into the lounge and wait for me. I'll be with you as soon as I can finish this call. There's coffee around the corner in the dining room if you'd like some. . . ."

"No thanks. I've had coffee up to here already." Andrea drew an imaginary line at nose level. "I'll just look around. Take your time."

She moved on into the comfortable lounge next to the office and glanced around curiously. Bookshelves flanked a big stone fireplace at one end of the long room, while glass display cases exhibited more of Graham's collection along the side walls. Crude stone weapons were cataloged on the nearest shelf, together with more sophisticated attempts at figure sculpture and assorted clay pots. Andrea's attention soon wandered to the metalwork in the next case. She was examining a large silver-colored plaque of religious figures when Graham came in.

"Boning up on your homework, eh?" he commented with a pleased smile. "You'll see lots better samples of this medium at the museum in town. All of us turn over the really fine pieces to them."

Andrea gestured toward the shelves. "You mean you're still uncovering these things?"

"You bet! A bunch of us have formed an exploration society down here in the southern part of the state. We go out into the hills every chance we get."

"But how do you know where to go?"

"There are always old maps and prospectors' stories to check out." He moved closer to her and pointed to another tablet. "That was unearthed sometime ago in a mountain cache east of Tumacacori."

"You've lost me already. . . ."

"Sorry. I forgot that you weren't familiar with our locations. Tumacacori's a National Monument now. The government preserved it as an example of mission architecture."

Andrea was still staring at the carving. "That looks like real silver. Isn't it terribly valuable?"

Graham shrugged. "You can't put prices on this kind of display."

"The workmanship is unusual. . . ." She bent over the case. "That bird symbol is really remarkable . . . there's so much depth to the design."

"It is interesting," he agreed. "We've found there's a definite market for reproductions of Indian art these days. The clay articles are especially easy to duplicate."

Andrea was puzzled. "For the ranch gift shop, you mean? I shouldn't think there would be enough business to warrant it."

"The shop here at the ranch is just a drop in the bucket. Roger exports all kinds of regional art objects to Europe. Some of his stuff comes up from Mexico, because they have a big labor market to supply inexpensive products."

"I had no idea it was such a big business."

Graham nodded. "His work here is just a sideline. The Circle C provides pleasant living quarters, so he can combine business and pleasure. Trust Roger to find the better parts of both worlds."

"And Françoise?"

Graham chuckled at her reserved tone. "She was probably too much for the family to handle at home. Actually, she's a good swimming coach when she puts her mind to it. If I have any trouble with her, I just get Roger or Steve to lay down the law." He moved over to the door, a stocky figure in his suntan slacks and red-checked shirt. "Let's go along if you're ready. I don't want to waste any of our day."

Andrea obediently followed him out under the shaded walkway to the parking lot for his car. "What do we do first?" she asked when he'd backed and turned down the road toward town.

"First, we go through the Archaeological Museum. Officially that's for your benefit, but actually it's a busman's holiday for me," he confessed. "Then we can drive out to the west side of town and visit the Desert Museum. That way you can see all the insects and snakes we have around here."

"Only if you promise they're in glass cases," she told him. "I was just congratulating myself on not having met any deadly creepy-crawlers so far."

"You needn't worry about that. The worst threat we've had this season is a ferocious frog who gets in the swimming pool every night. It's the truth," he said, as she started to laugh. "He thinks the whole pool is just for him. I haven't the heart to do more than scoop him out in the morning."

"I hope not." She relaxed on the seat. "All right, then —lead on. This should be fun."

The morning went by quickly despite its scholarly overtones. At the Archaeological Museum, Graham gave her a lighthearted but expert commentary on the extensive display, which included Indian artifacts from the entire Southwest. After their tour, they drove westward to the popular Desert Museum, set on the edge of the Saguaro

61

National Monument, where the tall cactus that was Arizona's symbol dotted the arid hillsides.

The museum itself was a modern building of native stone with displays that ranged from poisonous live snakes to a stuffed figure of the comical roadrunner. Very much alive were two incredibly ugly turkey buzzard chicks, who happily roamed the inner patio.

Andrea stared at them in fascination as she and Graham sipped coffee after lunch. The chicks wandered at will, seemingly enjoying the attention they were attracting. They were barely twelve inches high, but their big beaks and protruding eyeballs made them look like pocket-sized vultures. As they pecked gently at Graham's shoe-laces, they were as winsome and vulnerable as any young living creature.

"What a pity they can't stay this age forever," Andrea said thoughtfully. "They're certainly having a ball."

"It's a plush life," Graham agreed, "but you wouldn't care to supply their daily menu."

"Oh?" Her eyebrows rose. "Why not?"

"If we stick around a few minutes, you'll see. They like white mice—whole."

Andrea stared down at the black-and-white chick who was now pecking at the decorative buckle on her shoe. "Whole mice?" She shuddered. "Alive or dead?"

"Quite dead—but it wouldn't matter very much. The net result is the same for the mouse."

She pushed her coffee away. "I'm glad you didn't tell me before lunch."

He shrugged. "That's nature's law. The buzzards have as much right to live as the mice."

"I know, I know," she conceded, "but I'd just as soon skip feeding time if you don't mind."

Graham grinned and glanced at his watch. "There's still a while, so let me finish my coffee. I promise to change the subject," he added good-naturedly.

"All right. Let's get back to your hobby," she said, moving to a more comfortable position on the bench. "How do you know where to look on the treasure hunts?"

"Our main problem is deciding which of the maps are genuine. After that, we just follow instructions." He stared down into his coffee. "Most weekends are strictly pipe dreams—no treasure, but plenty of conversation and fun."

"You mentioned Tuma-something-or-other. Was it one of the big finds?"

"Tumacacori," he supplied easily. "Since it's a National Monument now, we can't poke around there anymore. It did cause a lot of excitement at one time, though."

"Tell me about it," she urged. "I think I could like this treasure hunting."

"Most people do. It's like one long scavenger hunt; not many of us can resist following the clues. The Tumacacori legend had its regiment of treasure seekers some years ago. Prospectors claimed the early padres had used the mission for extensive silver-mining operations. Unfortunately, they couldn't find any traces of the mine. By then the mission was abandoned and in ruins, but the prospectors were sure that the mission fathers had buried their treasures of silver and gold in the mountains west of Tumacacori before they went back to Spain. Everybody down here has been looking for it ever since."

Andrea leaned forward with interest. "Was it a very great treasure?"

"The story goes that they loaded three thousand burros with riches. Is that big enough for you?"

She whistled softly. "Sign me up as a new member of the club. Have they found any traces of it?"

"Not a smell. One legend says that the mission padres dynamited two mountain peaks over it. That makes the search take a little longer," he said solemnly.

"I see. In that case, I won't bother to stop and buy a shovel on the way back to the ranch."

"The Circle C will be happy to furnish a shovel anytime you want to dig up the countryside. Just don't disturb any of our fences, or I'll have Steve after my hide."

"Why? Is Mr. York difficult?"

"Steve?" Graham was vaguely puzzled. "Not really. He knows his business, that's all. We were certainly glad to finally hire an experienced foreman, because things were going downhill in that department. Now I don't have to worry about the outdoor part of the ranch and can concentrate on taking care of our guests instead."

"Which you do very nicely," Andrea hastened to assure him. Perversely, she went back to the other subject, although she was darned if she knew why. "What kind of background does Steve have?"

Graham grimaced. "The usual for that kind of work, I guess. Is it important?"

"Of course not—I was just being curious." She wrinkled her nose at him. "Terrible feminine habit."

He grinned at her teasing and then stood up. "You can be anything you want to with me, my dear. If we work our plans right, we could manage to have dinner away from the ranch, too. I know a place on the edge of town that makes a specialty of mesquite-broiled steaks."

Andrea stood up beside him and tightened her belt. "You're spoiling me. Perhaps we should go back to the ranch and see if anything needs your attention."

"What could be more important than picking a good place for dinner?" he asked, stepping aside to let her pass through the museum exit.

"Oh, I don't know. . . ." Her tone was purposefully vague. "Maybe there's been some sort of lead on Eric. . . ."

Graham stopped walking and stared down at her. "Now, how did you hear about him?"

"Did I let something out of the bag? I didn't mean to," she replied, wide-eyed. If Graham didn't know Eric was discovered on her porch, it wasn't the right time to volunteer the information. "Right now, I can't remember who told me about him," she went on. "I think some of the guests were concerned that he didn't stay in the hospital."

"Probably Ellie or that grandmother of hers," he deduced. "I was afraid there'd be trouble there. Eric knew better than to get serious about one of our guests." Graham put a hand under her elbow and moved on toward the parking lot. "There's a different set of rules for the ranch manager, though."

"I'll remember." She smiled up at him. "I have a sneaking suspicion you make your own rules."

"Feminine curiosity again?"

"Uh-huh. I must have an outsized lump of it." She paused by the car and waited for him to get out his keys, then nodded her thanks as he held open the door. "Whoosh . . . it's hot in here!" she exclaimed, getting in.

"Open the window for some ventilation. I'll have the air-conditioner going in a minute." Once he'd started the ignition and pushed a couple of levers, he asked, "How's that—better?"

Andrea sniffed the cold air gratefully as it emerged from a panel on the dashboard. "Marvelous. Too bad you can't install one of these on a horse."

"It would have saved you that sad experience with Hammerhead. Sure you don't feel any ill effects today?"

"Quite sure, thanks." She watched him maneuver among the parked cars before adding casually, "Actually, you could satisfy my curiosity if you would. Why is everybody so reluctant to talk about Eric? You'd think he had the plague or something."

He shot a somber look at her before focusing his attention on the road again. "Hardly, but almost as bad." His words came out in a resigned sigh. "I'm surprised you haven't guessed by now. The boy's coma, the erratic behavior at the hospital—all the rest. It was a drug overdose, of course."

"I see." Andrea swallowed hard and tried to hide the fact that she hadn't seen at all. Drugs had been the farthest thing from her mind. Alcohol . . . too much partying—her suspicions had moved along more conventional paths. The thought of that immature young man as a drug addict made her shudder visibly. No wonder Grandmaw Carter was determined to pry Ellie away from him.

"Don't take it so hard." Graham's voice finally penetrated her thoughts. "It's not unusual these days—you should know that, after living in Los Angeles. At least, that's what the newspapers tell us."

"Sorry to disappoint you, but some of us who live there still go along in the same old ways."

Her cool tone made him give her a rueful glance. "You don't disappoint me in the least. It's nice to hear there are still some sane people left. Sometimes I think they've been phased out."

"Heavens, don't surrender yet. There's quite a colony, but they don't make the headlines." The warmth came back to her voice. "Couldn't somebody have helped Eric before he got in this state?"

"He wasn't receptive for any therapy when I learned about his condition."

"Who told you about it?"

Graham's jaw firmed. "Steve. He felt it was his responsibility, since he'd hired him."

"And he didn't know about the drug habit?" There was skepticism in her words. "That doesn't seem likely."

"Maybe he didn't want to blow the whistle on him." Graham swung away from the center line to avoid an oncoming truck. "I told him yesterday that the boy would have to move on—that he couldn't come back after his stay in the hospital. We have our guests to consider first, so maybe it's just as well that he ducked out. At least it didn't come to a showdown over his job."

"But what will happen to him now?"

Graham shrugged. "Who can tell? Eric must have known the risks when he started the habit; now he'll suffer the consequences. Look, there's no point in ruining our afternoon with a grim subject like this. What about that steak dinner? We could take a run down to Tumacacori, and then come back to the eating place in town."

Andrea made a determined effort to shake off her depression. Graham was right; there was no point in spoiling the day.

"Your schedule sounds good," she said, turning to him with a smile, "but could we go back to the ranch first so I could change clothes? That turkey buzzard played havoc with my skirt hem when he nibbled on it."

Graham chuckled. "So that's why he was sticking so close to you."

"Probably he'd never seen pleats before," she told him cheerfully. "You don't mind going back to the ranch, do you?"

"I'm a little leery. Keep your fingers crossed that nothing urgent has come up while we've been gone."

Graham's hopes were dashed when they got back to his office. An unexpected Senior Citizens' tour group would like to arrive early the next morning and spend several days if the Circle C could accommodate them.

"Damn!" Graham said feelingly as he showed the telephone message to Andrea. "I knew I shouldn't have come back. This puts the kibosh on the rest of our day."

"Don't worry, there'll be others," she said. "Be happy that you have the extra bookings. Business wasn't too good, was it?"

"A little slow," he conceded. "This tour will help." He

66

scratched the back of his head. "Guess I'd better start ordering provisions."

"I'll leave so you can get to it. Thanks so much for the wonderful tour. I enjoyed it thoroughly."

"So did I." His gaze rested on her warmly. "Let's finish it properly at the first chance. All right?"

She smiled from the office doorway. "I'll hold you to it. Right now I have a date with the swimming pool, so I'll see you later."

Chapter FIVE

That pleasant interlude started the pattern for her holiday in the three days that followed. It was as if a storm cloud had suddenly passed over the Circle C, leaving the atmosphere clean and inviting after the initial disturbance.

The resort life ran as smoothly as travel brochures promise but seldom provide. Uninterrupted sunshine gave Andrea a fine excuse for relaxing on the side of the swimming pool, and Françoise even mellowed enough to utter grudging praise on her backstroke and offer excellent advice on her diving. In between, the Frenchwoman concentrated on perfecting her suntan in the most minuscule bikini allowed off the Riviera. The attention of all masculine guests, despite their ages or inclinations, was riveted on her each time she moved.

Grandmaw Carter commented on it one afternoon as she and Andrea sat under a sun umbrella at the pool's edge. "Graham'll have to raise that hussy's salary, the way she's acting. D'ya know that fool man from New Jersey is staying over three extra days?"

"Which man from New Jersey?" Andrea asked casually as she moved her legs out into the sunshine.

"The one wearing that purple getup. He's coming out of the dining room right now."

"What's wrong with staying three extra days?"

"Not a thing," the old lady said in a tart voice, "except that he spends all his hours right here at the swimming pool. I think he's waiting for something to happen every time Françoise steps on the diving board. It's downright disgraceful!"

Andrea tried to keep a straight face. "Well, nothing *has* happened yet. You'll have to give Françoise credit for that."

"She must have that blamed swimsuit sewed on,"

Grandmaw muttered. "In my day, a body would've been arrested. It's a good thing Ellie's not here...."

"Where is she?" Andrea was glad of an excuse to change the subject. "I thought we'd just missed each other at mealtime."

"Nope. She's off to a wedding in California. I told her mother not to hurry about letting her come back. It's a responsibility to raise a girl like Ellie nowadays."

"She seems pretty level-headed."

Grandmaw shrugged. "So-so. I'll think she's doing fine —then, the next minute she's in a tizzy over some new man. I wasn't sorry to see the back of Eric, I can tell you." Her finger stabbed the tabletop for emphasis. "Steve was a fool to keep him around as long as he did."

"I imagine Graham had the final say," Andrea offered diffidently.

Grandmaw made a rude noise with her lips. "How old are you, girl?"

"Twenty-five. Why?"

"You should be able to figure out who really runs this place. Graham doesn't spend much time on anything other than that hobby of his. That's why the owners are trying everything they can to get new guests. There's a mighty big investment here."

"If Graham's so ineffectual, how does he keep his job?"

"I didn't say there was anything wrong with him when you can get his attention." Grandmaw leaned back in her chair and squinted toward the sun. "He was smart enough to bring in Roger and Françoise . . . they're doing a good job. I saw you dancing with Roger last night. What do you think of him?"

It was Andrea's turn to be evasive. "He's a dandy dancer. . . ."

"A real specialist if he's as good on the dance floor as Françoise is in the swimming pool," Grandmaw said wryly. "But they're hardly what folks expect to find in a family resort."

Andrea grinned. "Maybe Graham's decided to change the Circle C's classification."

"Thank God the horses are still here. At least they don't change." The older woman peered sideways at Andrea. "How're you doing on top of Flathead?"

"You mean Hammerhead? We have a truce at the minute—I think I'm getting a little better."

"Does Steve let you go out alone on him?"

A bleak expression came over Andrea's face. "I haven't seen Mr. York for several days," she said carefully, looking down at her ankles. "Juan takes care of my riding. Yesterday he let me go out by myself, but only as far as the south gate. Today I thought I'd take the trail up to the cabin where they hold the cookouts." She nodded toward the Rincon foothills and then glanced at her watch. "I'd better get changed, or I'll run out of time and miss dinner."

"You taking Knucklehead?"

Andrea chuckled. "Poor Hammerhead. I suspect, though, that he's been called worse things."

"Yet bet he has! He's one of the most stubborn critters around." Grandmaw pursed her lips. "I wonder why Steve keeps you on him?"

Andrea stood up and pushed her chair against the table with a decisive gesture. "I told you—I haven't seen Steve York. He probably doesn't have the faintest idea what horse I'm riding . . . or even *if* I'm riding."

"Don't fool yourself, girl." Grandmaw shaded her eyes as she looked up at her. "There isn't anything around here that Steve doesn't keep an eye on. Sometimes I wonder why." Then, "Watch out for that Hammerhead, now."

"Chowderhead," Andrea said without thinking, and blushed furiously at Grandmaw's whoop of laughter.

She met Roger on her way to the stables a half-hour later. He looked agreeably surprised and pulled up in the middle of the path, blocking her way.

" 'allo, 'allo . . . what are you doing here? The swimming pool is behind you."

"So it is," she said, "but I don't go swimming in jeans. You're not as observant as usual. Late afternoon means horses on my schedule."

"I 'ave a different one," he informed her in his heavily accented English. "I've been down in Nogales arguing with my Mexican suppliers most of the day. The thought of a swim in the pool when I returned was the only thing that kept me from . . . how do you say it . . . ?"

"Blowing your top?"

He repeated the phrase thoughtfully and pursed his lips.

"Not bad. I must remember. Anyhow—now is the time to swim, and I need you." He flicked her shirt collar with his fingertip. "For company, *chérie*."

She edged away, carefully keeping her gaze at eye level, as Roger insisted on wearing his shirts practically unbuttoned to the waist. He certainly had no reason to complain of the heat, she decided, noting his expanse of hairy chest dubiously.

"Sorry—I have a date with my four-footed friend," she said. "It's the high point of his day. I can't disappoint him."

His forehead furrowed, then smoothed. "You mean that *diabolique* Hammerhead. Never mind—wait an hour. I'll come riding with you."

Andrea shook her head. "Nope. You're too good. I'd fall off if I tried to keep up with you. Hammerhead and I only know one speed—that's compound low."

"I don't understand." Roger ran an impatient hand through his already tousled hair. "What is thees compound low?"

"Slow," she replied succinctly. "Very slow. That's what Hammerhead and I do best." She shoved her hands in her jeans pockets and moved purposefully toward the stable. "I must go . . . I'm late now. Enjoy your swim, Roger."

"Wait! Promise me you'll be at the dance tonight."

Andrea smiled. "I'd love to."

"Then I'll let you go. If you come down early to dinner, there will be a martini waiting. . . ."

"Thanks, I'll remember. See you later." She gave him a brief wave before hurrying on down the path.

Hammerhead was waiting for her, saddled and tethered to the corral fence. At her approach, he lifted his head to bestow an unflattering glance before blowing rudely through his nostrils.

"Good afternoon to you, too, friend," Andrea told him austerely as she reached for the reins. "Now, stand still until I can get on you." She took advantage of a low rail on the fence to reach the stirrup. "How about that!" she said to the horse once she had managed to get up in the saddle. "Without help . . . would you believe it?" She glanced around hopefully for a wrangler to admire her prowess, but two bay horses down by the feeding trough were the only visible beings. "Guess we might as well go, chum," she finally instructed Hammerhead, nudging him gently with her heels. "Evidently I'm good enough to be left on my own."

Hammerhead snorted again as she turned him on a path leading toward the foothills.

"I wish you'd stop doing that. Your manners are terrible," she told him, wishing that she had somebody along who could hold up his end of the conversation more enthusiastically. When Juan had accompanied her, his teasing banter had helped her forget the temperature on their afternoon rides. Even Steve had managed some desultory comments that first day.

She scowled as she thought of the missing Mr. York. Her view of him locked in that embrace with Françoise had been the last glimpse she'd had. Pride had prevented her asking where he was in the days since. Now it seemed Juan was doing a disappearing act as well.

Sighing, she reached up and pulled her brimmed hat forward to shade her eyes more fully from the punishing sun. The desert landscape appeared quieter than usual as Hammerhead made his way stolidly up the narrow dirt trail into the government park tract. Towering green saguaro cacti dotted the ground on either side of her, looking like surrealistic creatures with their long-reaching arms and bulbous grooved cores. Mesquite and palo verde crowded between them to provide the main ground cover, while small patches of prickly pear and ocotillo would appear and disappear like Lewis Carroll's Cheshire cat.

Hammerhead stalked on with determination, kept from nipping tempting bits of greenery only by Andrea's equally determined grip on the reins. The path twisted around a low hill behind the ranch and then headed upward again.

Andrea squinted against the sun's glare to admire the rugged mountains ahead of her. Their rock outcroppings changed color as the afternoon shadows deepened —green merging with blue and then taking on a rich purple cast last of all in an extravagant display of natural beauty. She wished suddenly that she could preserve the scene . . . realizing the barren landscape touched the senses in a way that more lush scenery couldn't equal.

A cardinal fluttered overhead and then glided into the vegetation behind her.

"It's a good thing I'm not superstitious," Andrea told the

back of Hammerhead's ears. "A redbird is supposed to mean a visit from a stranger." She shifted in the saddle to look over her shoulder warily. "It's too deserted out here for entertaining company." She turned back and grasped the reins more tightly. "I think we'll take a quick look at that cabin where they're holding the cookout breakfast this weekend; then you and I will head for home."

Hammerhead dutifully quickened his steps. That last word had penetrated.

Andrea was hot and thirsty when the one-room stone cabin finally came into view. Juan had mentioned earlier that two canteens of water were kept in it to refresh riders on the hillside trail, and at the moment, the opportunity for a cool drink overshadowed her reluctance to enter the deserted structure. She urged Hammerhead up to the corner of the hut and dismounted.

"I won't be long," she advised him as she looked for a place to tie the reins. The best she could find was a spindly palo verde bush close to the back wall of the cabin. "You stay right here and behave yourself," she said, trying to remember how he'd been tied in the corral. At least her knit seemed secure, even if it wasn't a thing of beauty. Reaching up, she patted his dusty neck. "Remember to stand in the shade . . . and, if I know you, grab a bite while you're waiting."

Hammerhead peered around at her with his usual reproachful air. She laughed and gave him a final pat on the nose. "Five minutes, then we head back—if I can manage to crawl on top of you."

She needn't have worried. By the time she had entered the cabin, Hammerhead was investigating the tasty green shoots.

Andrea found two filled canteens just inside the door, as Juan had promised. While she stood drinking a cup of the cool water, she stared at the rough interior of the room. A black iron stove rested near one wall, and beside it there was a rectangular, wheeled barbecue. Two piles of stacking stools stood in a corner next to a shelf full of picnic gear. Andrea lifted a corner of the protective plastic covering and discovered neatly arranged paper cups and plates. Apparently the ranch chef merely brought in the perishable food; otherwise everything was already on hand for the weekly cookout.

She finished her water and tossed her styrofoam cup into a wastebasket. It would be nice if she could use a little more water to wash her face, but she decided against it. Someone might come along who really needed the precious liquid. She took a final look around the hut and then went out into the sunlight, closing the door carefully behind her.

A tiny horned toad was in the middle of the gravel path leading to the back of the building. Andrea stopped to kneel beside him and admire his brown-and-white camouflage, which blended so perfectly with the sandy ground. He stayed quietly by her boot, as if aware that he was in no danger. She smiled gently at the tiny creature, then straightened and went on around the building to retrieve her horse. "Are you ready to go home, boy?" she asked as she got around to the back. "I wasn't long, was I?"

There was no answering whicker, because there was no horse.

Andrea's mouth dropped open as she stared at the battered palo verde bush and the empty space in the landscape beside it.

"That miserable . . . lazy . . . conniving . . . no good . . . animal!" she muttered. "Going off and leaving me here! No wonder he was so placid . . . the horrible creature!" Grimly she moved over to the bush where she'd tied her missing steed and soon discovered how he'd worked his miracle. Apparently Hammerhead had simply eaten the branch for high tea, and then, finding himself free, had ambled off to find something choicer for dinner. Something like oats in the corral, she decided.

Andrea shook her head, amusement overcoming her initial irritation. Hammerhead had scored again! The fact that he'd left her with a four-mile walk back to the ranch hadn't touched his conscience in the least.

She moved back into the shade of the cabin to think things over. If she were to get back to the ranch in time for dinner, she should start walking now. On the other hand, if she waited an hour or so, the walk back would be considerably cooler and more comfortable. As far as food went, she could always scrounge something from the kitchen when she explained what had happened.

She tossed a mental coin and decided on the second course. If she took one of the stools from the cabin and

74

put it by the front door, she could get all the breeze that was going during her wait.

Once she'd arranged the stool, she was able to wedge herself comfortably against the doorjamb. Then she tilted her hat over her eyes and let her body relax. The ride had been warmer than she liked, and it was wonderful to feel the occasional whisper of wind on the open throat of her blouse. She undid another top button, her lips curving with amusement all the while. Roger's habit of dress must be catching, she mused, but at least she'd be cool while she waited. Her eyes drooped wearily, and gradually she stopped trying to keep them open.

"Have you decided to file squatter's rights on this place, or are you waiting for the cavalry to rescue you?"

The masculine voice sounded close beside her, and Andrea's eyes flew open to find Steve York surveying her with resignation. She jerked upright in alarm and would have tumbled off the stool if his hand hadn't clamped onto her shoulder.

"Take it easy, Miss Sinclair," he cautioned. "I didn't come out here to scare you to death." Seeing that she'd recovered her balance, he took his support away and reached for a cigarette in his shirt pocket. "You weren't really lost, were you?"

"Don't be ridiculous! Of course I wasn't." She shoved her hat back as she stared up at him, and then sprang to her feet as the realization of her position finally penetrated. "I was just waiting until . . . Oh!" Desperately she grabbed for him again as her leg folded under her.

"What's wrong?" For the first time there was alarm in his voice as he stared into her twisted face.

"My leg . . ." She winced when she tried to lower her foot. "It's full of pins and needles. I guess it was asleep."

"My lord!" Worry dissolved to an enigmatic expression. "I must be out of my mind."

"What do you mean by that?"

He didn't bother to answer, but merely bent over and scooped her up like a sack of feed. Without comment, she was carried over to the jeep he'd parked by the side of the building and dumped into the front seat.

"Where are you taking me?" she managed indignantly as he went around to get in on the driver's side.

"Now, where do you think?" His deep voice was pa-

75

tient, resigned. "Back to the ranch, of course. Unless you want to spend the night out here by yourself. Is that what you had in mind?"

"Certainly not. I wouldn't be here now if Hammerhead hadn't eaten his hitching post."

"Hell's fire! Don't you know enough not to tie that horse to anything edible?" He shook his head pityingly as he lit his cigarette. Then the ignition roared to life. "I thought Juan had gotten more across than that."

Andrea clung to the side of the jeep as they jounced onto the dirt track. "Don't blame it on Juan . . . it was my fault. I was just waiting at the cabin until the sun went down a little more. There wasn't any point in broiling on the walk back."

Steve flung her an approving glance. "It sounds as if you're learning, after all. I'm glad you told Grandmaw Carter where you were going, too. At least I knew where to start looking when Hammerhead came back without you. My main concern was that he'd thrown you off."

"Hammerhead? Don't be silly—it would require too much energy."

"That's why you're riding him. Believe it or not, he's the safest one in the string." Steve negotiated a dry wash before adding, "Next time, just don't tie him . . ."

". . . to anything he can chew. I know—I've learned my lesson." Her tone was preoccupied, because she was trying to button her shirt unobtrusively. "Thank you for coming after me so quickly."

"Don't be grateful . . . yet. Actually, I had an ulterior motive." He kept his gaze straight ahead, so he missed her sudden frown. "I could use your help with my job here."

"But I don't know a thing about guest ranches. Heavens, you should realize that by now. I've made every mistake in the book."

"Hold it." His hand came off the steering wheel to rest momentarily on her knee. "Let me finish. I'm not talking about ranch work. This is a special project. The first thing I want you to do when we get back is call your boss. He can give you the background. Don't mention it to anybody, and use the pay phone booth by the corral when you do your phoning."

"But why?" She turned to face him.

"I don't want the call going through the main switch-board." His hand moved back on the wheel as he continued in an impersonal tone. "If you're interested in helping me—after you've talked to your chief—meet me in town later tonight. All right?"

Andrea rubbed the side of her head wearily, wondering if she were hearing aright. "I think so. Wait, I just remembered . . . I told Roger I'd meet him at the dance tonight."

"That's all right. Keep the date. I can meet you later."

"Won't you be at the dance?" she wanted to know, thinking of his frequent appearances with Françoise.

"I don't know. If I do attend, it won't be for long."

"Just long enough to keep Françoise happy," she probed bitterly.

This time he did look amused, although his eyes merely flicked over her. "Something like that. I didn't know it bothered you."

"It doesn't." She matched his casual response. "You haven't mentioned how I'm supposed to get to town after the dance. I can hardly ask Roger to give me a ride."

"I wouldn't recommend it," he said dryly. "Call a rental agency and have a car delivered. They can park it behind your cottage; nobody will think anything about that. If they do, tell them you plan to use it for sightseeing."

She sighed. "It seems like a lot of cloak-and-dagger stuff to me. You're sure this is necessary?"

Steve turned up the lane to the back of the corral and pulled the jeep into a shaded parking space before answering. "I wouldn't be doing it otherwise." He kept his voice low. "I'll meet you at a Mexican restaurant in town called El Torito at eleven o'clock. Don't say anything about going . . . understand? That's important."

She put one leg on the ground, then shifted to tell him, "You don't have to keep going on about it. You've made your point."

"I hope so." He remained in the driver's seat and returned her look with a bleak stare. "And I hope to God I'm doing the right thing."

Her countenance became thoughtful. "Is it so vital?"

"Damned right. We don't play for wooden matches." He raised his voice deliberately. "I'm glad you weren't hurt, Miss Sinclair. You'll have to be more careful with that

77

horse on the next ride. If you hurry, you'll still be in good time for dinner."

Andrea obediently picked up his cue. "Thanks again for the rescue. Oh, could you lend me a dime? I didn't bring my coin purse with me."

Gravely she watched him extract one from a pocketful of change.

"Is that all you want?" he asked.

She smiled sweetly. "For the moment, Mr. York, I think that's quite enough." She marched purposefully toward the phone booth without looking back.

CHAPTER SIX

The El Torito restaurant was located in an unprepossessing one-story building on Tucson's east side. Andrea parked her rental car as close to the entrance as possible in the shadowed and sparsely used parking lot, reflecting that Steve certainly hadn't selected the most popular place in town. She sat quietly in the front seat for a minute after she had removed the ignition key, strangely reluctant to enter the building and take up her job in earnest. For a job was what it was, she told herself. Had been ever since she had talked to her office in Los Angeles.

"I can't force you to help him, Andrea," her chief had said over the phone, "but it would certainly make it easier for me if you would. Cooperating with government agencies is necessary in this business. . . ."

"But *what* government agency," Andrea broke in. "You'll have to start from the beginning . . . Steve didn't tell me anything."

"Get *him* to do the explaining; they don't go around opening their files to strangers. All I learned was that York's presence at the ranch is official, and any help you can give him will be appreciated. That's a direct quote, in case you're interested."

Andrea had sighed and clutched the receiver tighter. It was stuffy in the phone booth, and an inquisitive fly was dive-bombing her head, but she persisted, nonetheless. "Okay . . . so I'll cooperate. What in the dickens are they hunting for—hoof-and-mouth disease?"

There was a puzzled silence at the other end of the wire. Then, "You've got the wrong government department, honey. Men from the Bureau of Dangerous Drugs aren't worried about things walking around on four legs . . . just two."

At his words, the pieces of the puzzle fell abruptly into place for Andrea. Eric's disappearance, and Steve's reluctance to mention it, suddenly made sense. Like most Americans, her knowledge of people who worked for the Bureau of Dangerous Drugs was hazy. Steve would answer most of her questions, although instinctively she knew that he wouldn't volunteer any information.

Her chief concluded by saying enviously that "it sounded as if she were getting a lot more excitement on her vacation than he could expect on his." Her reply was noncommittal as she replaced the receiver. Steve's expression when he had said "We don't play for wooden matches" wasn't the look of a man who thoroughly enjoyed his work.

With a strange feeling of reluctance, Andrea pulled open the door of the restaurant. Inside, the decor surprised her; it was surprisingly luxurious, with a deep-piled carpet and a bar done in green leather along the wall to the right. Beyond the bar, the overhead lighting stopped, and the restaurant tables were illuminated only by hurricane lanterns. Bouquets of brightly colored straw flowers were everywhere in the intricately decorated tin containers.

An attractive hostess whose black hair was in two long braids came up to Andrea. "Miss Sinclair . . ." She barely waited for Andrea's nod before saying, "This way, please. The gentleman is waiting for you." Walking with a graceful carriage, she led the way to the dining room, threading her way among the tables until she reached a banquette at the rear.

Steve, conservatively dressed in a gray business suit, rose as she approached, and moved down on the upholstered bench to make way for Andrea.

"You're right on time," he said with approval.

Andrea nodded, her glance following the hostess, who had gone back to her place by the cashier. "How did she know where to bring me? . . . I didn't even have a chance to ask for you."

"Nothing difficult about that—I just told her to watch for a hot-tempered blonde wearing a coat."

"That's not fair, I'm not . . ." Her denial trailed off under his amused glance. "Well, at least I'm not wearing a coat."

"So I notice." His eyes moved appraisingly over her black chiffon, which had soft dolman sleeves and a high

80

neck but practically no back. "Very nice. Quite a change from this afternoon. If you'd had that rig on, Hammerhead certainly wouldn't have run away." He waited for her to sit down and then settled easily beside her. "Did you have any trouble getting here?"

Andrea put her purse down on the bench beside her, keeping a discreet ten inches between them. "No trouble. My boss told me to look for the man in the white hat."

"Haven't you heard—these days there are no white hats and no black ones! Everything's just a blob of gray."

She shook her head. "Don't you believe it! There are a lot of people who still feel the way I do—we don't like compromising on principle." Her gaze became quizzical. "I didn't think you'd be apologizing for your work."

"Who the devil's apologizing!" It was the old Steve again, despite his conventional clothing. "If I didn't believe in what I was doing, I sure as hell wouldn't be here." He caught her flicker of a smile. "And you can stop leading me on, Miss Sinclair. If you're going to work with me, the first thing you have to learn is who's boss."

"I haven't signed a contract yet. How's the pay?"

"Nonexistent for you." His eyes crinkled with amusement. "You get the department's fervent thanks and then go back to Los Angeles and forget all about it."

"Well . . ." She pretended to consider.

"I didn't think you'd need to be paid for hanging around Roger Villier," he went on. "Lots of women do that for free."

"Is *that* what I'm supposed to do?" Her disappointment was evident.

"You're not signing on for the duration—strictly temporary help," he said, lifting his eyebrows. Then, in an aside, "Here comes the waitress. I hope you like Mexican food."

"Just so it's *tacos* and *frijoles refritos*," she told him after peeking at the huge menu he had opened.

"Sounds good—make that two," he told the waitress, who was dressed in a peasant blouse and colorful skirt. "Beer, I think." He glanced questioningly at Andrea. "All right with you?"

"Fine, thanks."

"Two glasses of beer. We'll decide on dessert later." He watched the girl move off to place their order.

Andrea reached out and pushed the hurricane lantern away from the cutlery and napkins. "They must save a whale of a lot of money on electricity in this place."

He looked amused. "That's one of the side benefits. You're supposed to appreciate the romantic atmosphere. Later on, they have some strolling mariachi musicians."

"Did you pick it for that reason?" she asked hopefully. Perhaps the man *did* have a personal side, after all.

"My lord, no. I was trying to find a place where we wouldn't be seen. You can't find anybody in here unless you carry a flashlight."

"Oh." He needn't have been so vehement about it, she decided. Straightening her shoulders, she said coolly, "In that case, maybe we'd better get down to business. I've agreed to help, but I *would* like to know a little of the background . . . if it's possible."

"Sounds fair enough." He was ignoring her sarcasm. "I can give you some of the facts—all you'll need to know." He half-turned to face her, resting one broad shoulder against the upholstered bench back. "You've probably read about the problem this country is having with drug infiltration from Mexico?"

"A little. Don't they call it the 'new Acapulco gold'?"

"Among other things. I know a better name." There was a grimness in his voice. "My department tries to stop the flow into the United States."

"But I thought most of the drug traffic was through Canada."

He frowned. "If you want statistics, I can furnish a few. Eighty percent of the heroin used in white suburbs of this country comes from Mexico. Since there's only twenty-seven miles of fenced border between El Paso and the Pacific Ocean, it makes our job rough. Then add a lesson in basic finance—when a smuggler pays twenty thousand dollars for a buy of marijuana in Mexico, he can usually sell it for one hundred thousand when he gets it to a major market in the States. That makes our job rougher. Want to hear more?"

She nodded.

"Okay." He grinned slightly. "But you asked for it." In a more serious tone, "So, even though our men cooperate with the U.S. Customs people at the border and work

82

with the Federal Judicial Police in Mexico, we wouldn't have a prayer unless we obtained information in other ways. We rely on informants generally, but that's not how this job started."

"Wait a minute—how does Roger Villier come into it?"

"I'm getting to that." He noted a girl coming toward them. "Here's the waitress with our beer. Would you like a cigarette to go with it?"

"Please." She watched him fish out his pack, took a cigarette, and waited while he lit a match from the souvenir box on the table. "Thanks."

"Now, then . . ." He nodded his thanks to the waitress and took a sip from his frosty pilsener glass. "We heard about Roger first from the Customs people—he was crossing the border more than the average number of times. The next step was a check on his bank account, and that's where we got our first surprise. He had savings accounts scattered in San Diego, Los Angeles, and Phoenix showing sizable balances. All the accounts had been opened by mail, and hefty cash deposits were made the same way."

"Why should that put him under surveillance? He represents a big import firm in France—Graham told me about it."

"He probably didn't tell you that the Villier headquarters is in Marseilles. The main drug route to this country runs Marseilles, Montreal, and then Vancouver. Another big routing goes from Marseilles to Mexico. Roger's family firm has been under suspicion by the French authorities for some time. His presence down here seems too coincidental to us."

She frowned. "How do you know about the international angle of this? I thought narcotics men concentrated on local use."

"Not any longer. The ramifications are too big for one nation alone. Our bureau has one hundred twenty-five men working in over forty of our embassies abroad . . . cooperating with foreign law-enforcement agencies."

"Well, you fooled me. I thought you were strictly a dude-ranch foreman." Her chin went up as she gave him a searching look. "You certainly pretended to know everything about the job."

"I *do* know quite a bit," he pointed out mildly. "Anyhow, enough to satisfy Graham and the owners of the Circle C. I was telling the truth about that ranch in Colorado."

"Then they don't know about the other part of your work?"

He made a decisive gesture. "Hell no! Nobody does . . . except Juan. He's a member of the bureau, too. You're a calculated risk," he added dispassionately. "I need a cover when I go to Nogales in a day or so, and you seem to get on well with Roger Villier."

She pulled the ashtray to her and stubbed out her cigarette with more force than was absolutely necessary. "You aren't doing badly with Françoise—or is that business?"

He sat back and grinned. "She comes under that general heading. In her case, the fringe benefits are pleasant."

"You mean you want to keep an eye on her?"

"Oh, absolutely," he drawled.

"Really!"

Immediately his expression sobered. "Now, look, Andy—"

"Don't call me 'Andy'!"

"Sorry." He didn't sound the least remorseful as he went on, "All you have to do . . . Andrea . . . is to keep your eyes open when you're around Roger. Accept any invitations that he hands out. Did anything come from the dance tonight?"

"Not really. He talked casually about our having coffee tomorrow." She grimaced. "*If* he has time between checking some shipments."

"He's not the only one who's checking. We've already been through the stuff."

"And there's nothing?"

"One gross of souvenir items, as ordered. Nothing more." He paused and said, "Here comes our food. Let's forget business for a while and enjoy ourselves."

Andrea was pursuing the last bite of her *frijoles* a little later when she glanced up to find him staring at her. "I'm sorry to take so long," she apologized. "Everything tasted so good that I hated to leave any of it."

"Stop fussing. I'm glad to see that Hammerhead hasn't

ruined your appetite. How do you like life at a guest ranch, by the way?"

"Fine." She took a swallow of beer before going on. "Ummm . . . that's better. My mouth feels like a bed of coals. You should have warned me."

"I couldn't," he said laconically. "I've never been here before."

His remark cheered her strangely. All evening she had envisioned Françoise on a similar date, and the illusion had rankled.

"That was a pretty terse answer to my question," he pointed out, "or were you simply being diplomatic?"

"No, I just had to put out the conflagration first." She gave him her full attention. "Really, I've had a fine time this week, and, to be honest, I didn't expect to. The great outdoors is new to me."

"Comes from living in cities all your life." He pushed his empty plate away and rested a forearm on the table. "Nothing like sniffing fresh air for a change."

"How do you know where I've lived?" she asked, frowning.

"We can't afford to work in the dark with our people. I can tell you what languages you speak, how you're five minutes late to work in the mornings but generally stay twenty minutes over at night to make up for it. I know your major in college, when you had your teeth straightened, and the current status of your love life."

"You've a colossal nerve—"

"Don't fly off the handle again. Think about it, and you'll realize why we have to be thorough. Besides, you haven't anything to be ashamed of. Take that fellow you were dating last year . . ."

Her eyes widened. "Has he done something wrong?"

"Not that I know of." Steve sounded amused. "Apparently he hasn't done anything to raise his blood pressure in thirty years. The report was mighty dull."

"I could have told you that and saved you the trouble," she said, putting her fork down on the edge of her plate. "Since you know all the answers, I'm surprised you're still asking questions. Have you even learned what I wear to bed? . . ."

"Green nylon with a bunch of ruffles over the shoulder."

She flared immediately. "I think it's a disgrace to waste the taxpayers' money for plain monkey business."

His deep laugh interrupted her. "Andy . . . Andy . . . you'll never learn." He was shaking his head. "You explode like a skyrocket. . . ."

"Stop calling me 'Andy'!"

"Sorry, *Miss* Sinclair. You can relax about the clothes. I was in your room after you passed out with sunstroke . . . remember? The taxpayers haven't lost a penny on your wardrobe, nighttime or otherwise."

"Now you've made me feel more of a fool than usual," she confessed. "Just the way I felt this afternoon when I let Hammerhead run away from me. I should have known better."

"Trying to outsmart that horse is an impossibility," he drawled. "Like hoping to find a white blackbird or an experienced kamikaze pilot. Hammerhead's an established institution on the Circle C."

"You really like the life there, don't you?"

"It's a nice change from my work," he admitted.

"Is it hard to get a job with your department?" When he frowned at her query, she went on hastily, "I really want to know—I'm not being nosy." Then sheepishly, "Not really nosy."

He grinned at her attempt to be honest. "Okay. Since we called you into this—you do have a right to be filled in on the background. Our department's strictly civil service, Miss Sinclair. These days they prefer agents with college degrees in law or political science. After the applicant takes the written examination, there's an oral panel, and then a rigid physical."

"A practically perfect speciman?" she teased.

His eyebrows went up slightly. "Hardly. Let's just say there can't be any arrests or drug use in the applicant's background."

"What comes next?"

"Successful applicants are sent to a ten-week agents' school in Washington, D.C., where they're taken in hand by Marine Corps drill instructors to polish their specialties."

"And when you're graduated, you're one of the Narcs," she finished smugly.

He shook his head. "Sorry to disillusion you, but the

Narcs are the men assigned to the narcotics detail of the local law-enforcement people. If you're going to get your slang right—we're called the Feds. The informers we use are known as snitches or stools." He chuckled at her chagrined expression. "Don't worry, you're doing fine. The main thing to remember is that this bureau works undercover more than any other agency involved in this work."

"I see," she said somberly. "Do you always work with Juan?"

"No, although two agents are always assigned to a case—never just one. They, in turn, work with eight to ten other agents, who report to a supervisor."

"Here in Tucson?"

"Our headquarters for this area is in Denver." Absently he put his napkin on the table. "I just got back from there, but that's not common knowledge."

"So you were out of town." She shook her head deprecatingly. "I imagined you were avoiding me."

He gave her a strange look. "Now, why would I do that?"

"I don't know . . . except that you were so thick with Françoise . . . or at least that's how it seemed." She waited for him to comment, but when he didn't, she added feebly, "And I'd already been such a terrible nuisance."

"Not too bad," he reassured her blandly. "You'd impressed me enough to have a background check run on you so I could enlist your help."

"Really?" Her heartbeat speeded at his unexpected praise.

"Absolutely. Any woman who'd risk sunstroke rather than admit she couldn't take it sounded right for this job."

"Oh." The heartbeat went back to its plodding ways. She'd been right the first time; Steve was thinking only of the job. Deliberately, she bunched her napkin and put it on the table. "We'd better be going . . . unless you want to tell me more about the trip to Nogales and what I'm suppose to do there."

"There'll be plenty of time for that later on." He picked up the check and was reaching for his wallet. "All we have to do now is get back to the ranch without being seen together. Will you give me a lift? . . . I didn't bring a car with me."

"Of course. There shouldn't be any trouble . . ." She broke off at his sudden frown, "What's the matter?"

"Listen!" He made a brief, shushing motion with his hand. "That sounds like Grandmaw Carter. Damn! You can hear her coming a block away." He picked up the oversized menu from the edge of the table and opened it in front of them. "Move closer to me," he told Andrea peremptorily. "Quick! And keep your head down!" He encircled her shoulders with his free arm, pulling her tight against him on the bench. "That's it."

Andrea held her breath, not daring to look up as a party of people went by. It was easy to overhear Grandmaw's pungent comments about the crowded tables, as the older woman's voice penetrated like sand in a hardboiled egg.

Steve finally raised his head slightly and then loosened his grasp on her shoulders. "They're going into the next room. She's with Graham and somebody else. Do you recognize him?"

Andrea peered through the shadowed room and caught a profile glimpse. "No, I don't think so. Oh, wait a minute . . . he's the man from the museum. I'm almost sure of it. Graham introduced me when we looked at the archaeology collection the other day. What's the matter?" she asked as Steve uttered an impatient exclamation.

"Next I'll be trying to find something suspicious in the bingo game they hold at the ranch. For a minute there, I thought that Graham and Grandmaw were an unlikely pair for a night out. . . ."

Andrea shook her head. "Not really. Ever since Ellie's been gone, the poor soul has been lonely. She probably leaped at the chance to get away."

"Sounds reasonable. There's probably a good reason for the museum fellow, too."

"I'm afraid so. They sounded like good friends when Graham introduced me the other day. This archaeological society that he belongs to has furnished quite a bit of the museum's permanent collection. Look, do we have to stay hunched over like this? I'm getting a crick in the neck or something."

"Sorry." Steve took another cautious glance over the top of the menu before he closed it and tossed it back on the tabletop. "I think the all-clear has sounded. That's unless we have the bad luck to meet Roger coming in the front door when we're leaving."

"He didn't say anything about it at the dance."

"Ummm. That's something." He stood up. "Sorry to cheat you out of dessert, but we'd better get out of here while we're ahead. Maybe we can stop off on the drive back to the ranch."

She wriggled out from behind the table and stood beside him. "Whatever you say. It's a good thing we're leaving. If we'd huddled behind that menu much longer, we'd have had to order something."

Steve moved aside for her to precede him once they reached the foyer. "Go on out to your car while I'm paying . . . the sooner we separate, the happier I'll be."

Andrea knew he was thinking of the security angle, but she felt a twinge all the same. She managed a thin smile. "All right . . . I'll wait in the parking lot. Should I have the motor running?"

"Not unless you want to start the air-conditioner."

"I was thinking of a fast getaway. . . ."

He paused before they reached the cashier's cage. "Deliver me from gifted amateurs. I'd be happier if you stop treating this like a sequel to *Bonnie and Clyde*."

She raised her eyebrows. "No sense of humor."

"None."

"Okay . . . but it'll never sell at the box office." For the cashier's benefit, she patted his coat sleeve and added, "thanks so much for dinner. It was nice seeing you again, Uncle Steve. G'night." She watched a surge of red go up the back of his neck and felt a perverse satisfaction as she went out into the night.

When Steve joined her at the car a few minutes later, he gave her a cold look. "Your background notes didn't list the dramatic touch. What's with the 'Uncle Steve' business?" he growled.

"That's to throw anyone who's following us off the track," she said brightly, turning the ignition key. "I thought it was a nice touch."

He got in and slammed the door. "Do me a favor, will you?"

"Of course." She turned eagerly to face him. "What?"

"From now on, stop thinking."

"Oh." She lowered her eyes to hide her sudden chagrin.

"Sorry, I guess this whole thing doesn't seem very real to me."

"Let's hope it stays that way." He glanced around the quiet parking lot. "Take off, will you?" As she eased away from the parked cars and turned right down a brightly lighted Speedway Boulevard, he asked, "Do you want to stop somewhere for coffee?"

"No thanks. After all the excitement today, I don't need any coffee to stay awake."

She drove along the broad street without further conversation for several blocks. Finally she couldn't stand it any longer. "When do we make the trip to Mexico?"

"Any day now." His tone was preoccupied.

Andrea saw he was staring straight ahead, his long fingers stroking the side of his jaw.

"I wonder . . ." he said eventually.

She slowed for a dip in the road. "What now?"

"Why Graham is so fascinated with this museum business? You'd think he'd spend more time on the ranch."

Andrea thought it over for a minute. "I don't see the conflict. What's wrong with meeting a friend for something to eat? These aren't exactly working hours . . . for most people, anyhow." She increased the car's speed and went on, "Maybe Grandmaw Carter set up the date. Graham said they could use some new members in their society, and Grandmaw would have a handy bankroll to contribute. That would explain the museum man's being there, too. Maybe Graham wanted him to explain how successful they've been."

"In what way?"

She could feel him turn toward her on the seat, but resolutely kept her eyes on the traffic. "They've sold reproductions of the original finds. You can buy them at the museum, and it's hard to tell them from the original articles. Honestly, you should take a look at them . . . the carving detail is terrific."

"Maybe I will."

"The fellow at the museum would like to have all of Graham's collection. You know, the pieces he has displayed in the lounge—but Graham isn't about to part with them."

"They must be pretty valuable."

"To another collector," she agreed, stopping at a red

light and glancing across at him. "Southwest Indian stuff isn't in the Rembrandt category."

"I'll take your word for it. S'funny that Roger doesn't stock museum reproductions in the gift shop."

"Probably the ranch guests would rather buy towels with roadrunners on them, and desert mosaics. They're certainly easier to pack in a suitcase."

"I meant to ask where you finally stowed that coat of yours."

The darkness provided a welcome cover for her sheepish expression. "I hoped you'd forgotten that."

He chuckled and settled comfortably back on the seat. "I haven't forgotten anything." There was an instant's pause before he added, "Maybe that's the trouble."

"I wish you'd stop being so mysterious."

He ignored her complaint. "Take it easy when you turn into the ranch road . . . it's full of potholes. We've told the county to get busy and repair it."

Andrea had managed the dirt road easily on her way to town, and felt like telling him so. Either Steve was one of those males who had to instruct a woman how to handle a car, or he was deftly changing the subject. Since he was still slouched on the seat, the latter possibility made more sense.

"Where do you want me to drop you?" she asked finally, when they were nearing the main gate to the ranch.

"Take the back road on up to your cottage," he commanded. "Park right behind it. I'll walk back down."

"There's no need . . . I can drop you closer to your quarters than that."

"Stop arguing," he said mildly, "and remember, you drove back to the ranch alone . . . in case anyone asks. Incidentally, what reason did you give for going into town?"

"Nose drops," she said glibly, and indicated her purse with one hand. "I even stopped and bought a bottle. This dry air is a shock to my sinuses after the Los Angeles smog."

He frowned. "I'm sorry to hear that."

"For heaven's sake, I'm just fooling. My sinuses are fine . . . so far as I know. I needed a cover story for Roger." She clung to the wheel as the car jounced on the rough surface of the lane that led in behind her cottage.

Finally she sighed in relief as she was able to pull up and park.

"It's a wonder he didn't want to go with you."

She shook her head. "That's all you know about it. If you want to see men scatter, reach for a handkerchief and start talking about symptoms."

"I'll remember. Get out your side, and I'll slide across after you—in case someone's listening," he added, as she stared at him.

"Do you really think someone around here suspects you?" she whispered.

"Why take chances? Come on, I'll see you safely inside."

Darkness enveloped them as they moved around the cottage. Down the hillside, the swimming pool was outlined with colored lights, and hooded bulbs marked path boundaries, but otherwise the ranch was completely cloaked by the desert night.

The noise of their footsteps seemed unnaturally loud on the stone porch of the cottage, and Andrea found herself walking on tiptoe when they reached the door. Inevitably her glance flickered toward the wall where Eric's body had lain. This time, the space was reassuringly empty, but, as if diagnosing her thoughts, Steve wordlessly held out his hand for her key. Still without speaking, she gave it to him and moved inside as soon as he'd opened the door.

She waited until he'd closed it behind him before she reached around and turned on the light switch. "It's all right," she said, forestalling any objection. "I pulled the curtains before I left. No one will know that I have company." She moved across to put her purse on the desk. "Will you sit down, or did you just come in to look under the bed for me?"

"Naturally I'll be glad to check under the bed if you're nervous," he said calmly.

"Who's nervous?" Then, before he could answer, "All right . . . I guess I am, a little."

He grinned. "Look, Andy . . . I didn't sign you up to play Mata Hari. All you have to do is stick close to Roger and see what's going on."

"I wish you'd stop calling me that." Her objection

sounded automatically, but it lacked fire. "I've been thinking . . ."

He looked up from his examination of the plaque on the mantel. "That *could* be dangerous."

She waved that aside airily. "Why would Roger be such a fool as to put those savings accounts in his own name? I certainly wouldn't . . . if I had anything to hide."

"You might. Remember, the accounts aren't in Tucson. They're scattered around."

"What address did he give?"

"Blind post-office-box numbers—nothing that could be traced there." Steve ran his finger over the face of the plaque. "I hadn't realized they'd scattered this stuff around the cottages for decoration." He turned it over and surveyed it casually. "Good backing, so you can use it for hanging, too."

"I know." She put it back on the mantel after he'd handed it to her. "I'll have to buy one before I leave." Absently she traced one of the carved birds. "Do you know how long that will be?"

"Not long for you." He shoved his hands in his coat pockets, looking tired and dispirited. "If you stayed too long, everybody would be suspicious. You'll have to go back home on time."

"That just gives me the rest of the week." She moved over to turn down the air-conditioning unit so that the hum was not so pronounced. "I'll do my best, but Roger isn't the type to be bowled over. Remember, he's been living around Françoise."

"That has the earmarks of a dirty crack. What's the matter—don't you like our swimming instructor?"

She blinked innocently. "We're crazy about each other. I just stay out of the pool when I'm alone with her because deep water frightens me. Anything else you want to know?"

His slanted grin turned to a frown as they heard a knock on the door.

"Who can that be?" she whispered.

His eyebrows went up cynically. "Not expecting anybody?"

"Of course not," she hissed. "Did you think I sent out invitations for an open house?"

The knock was repeated before Steve could answer.

Then Roger's voice came from outside. "Andrea . . . come out . . . come out, *mignonne*." His knuckles beat a determined tattoo on the door.

"What shall I do?" Andrea whispered, turning toward Steve with a stricken expression.

He shoved her gently toward the door, keeping his hand on her bare back. "Don't open it," he murmured. "Ask him what he wants."

She nodded and waited until the fusillade of knocking stopped. "Roger?" She put her mouth close to the wood panel. "What do you want?"

"Ah, *chérie!* Let me in, will you?"

Steve's strong fingers exerted a warning pressure on her shoulder blade.

"Sorry, Roger . . . I can't," she said obediently. "I was just getting ready for bed. That's why I took so long getting to the door. Was it something special?"

"I came to invite you to go swimming." His voice sounded truculent. "Do I 'ave to stand out here and shout at you?" There was a pause before he added, "Come on, *chérie.* It's a beautiful night, and we'll 'ave the pool to ourselves. Everyone else has gone to bed."

Andrea looked inquiringly over her shoulder. Steve scowled and then shook his head. "Tomorrow," he mouthed.

Her eyebrows went up, but she turned back to the door. "Roger . . . I can't. I've shampooed my hair and just finished putting it up. Could I take a raincheck on your invitation tomorrow . . . please? I'm so sorry."

Evidently her regretful wail was convincing, because he finally said grudgingly, "All right . . . tomorrow then. I don't know why you have to keep the door closed . . . I 'ave seen women before with wet hair. Françoise spends half her time that way."

Andrea fumed as she heard the stifled chuckle behind her. "Sorry . . . I prefer privacy."

"All right, *ma mie.* Tomorrow, then . . . when your hair is dry."

"To go swimming?"

"*Mon Dieu* . . . no!" He raised his voice. "Why would you get your hair wet when you finally get it dry? Then you would want to lock yourself away in your room again. I'm talking about going riding after breakfast. *Très bien?*"

Andrea glanced up at Steve and saw his nod. "Fine," she called through the door. "I'll look forward to it. Will you ask them to get the horses ready?"

"Of course . . . leave it to me. It will do York good to have something to do. He doesn't work any harder than Eric did."

This time it was Andrea who stifled the chuckle as she felt Steve's body stiffen at the slur.

"You're right," she said silkily. "The fellow's a terrible goof-off. I'm surprised he gets away with it."

Roger mumbled something indistinguishable. Apparently he wasn't interested in discussing their foreman's virtues. He went back to the only subject that concerned him. "Till tomorrow, then—if you're late for breakfast, I'll come pound on this door again."

"Don't worry . . . I'll be ready."

"Bien! Bonne nuit, chérie."

"Good night, Roger . . . and thank you." As the Frenchman's steps retreated from the porch, Andrea pulled away from Steve's hand and rested her shoulders against the cool wood of the door panel. The nerve ends where his fingers had touched her still quivered. She drew a deep breath to steady her palpitating insides and asked, "Well, how did I do?"

"Not bad . . . for a beginner." He seemed amused. "Roger wasn't impressed with your excuse for the locked door."

"Maybe it was something new for him."

"Which? Excuses or locked doors?" He pushed her away from the door as methodically as he would have moved a chair that was in the way. "You didn't tell me you'd made such a conquest. Maybe you can get some information out of him after all."

Andrea was stung by his dispassionate appraisal. "In that case, why didn't you let me go on the swimming date with him tonight? Why wait until tomorrow?"

Steve's jaw settled in grim lines. "Whatever he had in mind tonight wouldn't have helped my case. All I did was save you from a mauling."

"Oh, for heaven's sake . . . I can take care of myself!" she began angrily.

He jerked the door open. "Then I suggest you save your strength. You'll need it in the morning."

She followed him through the doorway and said, "He certainly wouldn't try anything in broad daylight."

Steve hesitated on the porch step, looking back over his shoulder. "That's what you think. Watch out, or he'll have you on the ropes again!"

"Roger?" Her voice was incredulous.

His shoulders shook with sudden laughter. "Who's talking about Roger? I meant Hammerhead." Still chuckling, he added, "Now, get some sleep . . . I'll see you in the morning."

Chapter SEVEN

Despite his promise, Steve didn't appear in the dining hall the next morning. Grandmaw Carter sat ensconced at her end of the table and surveyed Andrea's riding gear with interest. Françoise, sitting two places away, bestowed a cursory glance and went back to chewing a piece of toast.

Grandmaw waited until Andrea had ordered before probing delicately, "I didn't know you'd signed up for the morning rides."

Andrea looked up from her tomato juice, startled. "I haven't. I mean, today's the first time."

"The morning ride's the fast ride." Grandmaw made it sound like the end of the world was coming. "I didn't think you were good enough for that."

"She isn't," Françoise said from the sidelines. "Roger's invited her." Her tone indicated that the end of the world was probably a good thing, since it was going to hell in a handbasket anyhow. "They aren't going for a ride . . . he plans to walk the horses all the way."

"Why should he do that?" Andrea asked. "I'm not *that* bad anymore. Juan's been coaching me."

Françoise shrugged. "Ask Roger. All I know is what he told me." She stabbed her toast into her coffee, like a stiletto. "You can do more things on a horse when he's just walking," she added unexpectedly.

Andrea choked on a swallow of juice as she stared at the other woman. "Just what do you have in mind?"

Françoise blinked. "Don't you know?" She glanced down at Grandmaw Carter. "Perhaps in thees country women do not approve . . ."

"Go right ahead and talk." The gray-haired woman waved a benevolent hand. "I'm old enough to listen. You foreigners must be ahead of us in some things. It's a good

97

thing Ellie isn't here, though, or I'd have to send her away from the table."

"Oh, for heaven's sake—" Andrea began.

"Well, if you really want to know," Françoise interrupted, giving them an irritated look, "Roger said—"

"Good morning, good morning. Sorry to be late." Graham breezed in and pulled out the chair next to Andrea. He sat down and glanced at the menu card, asking, "Have I missed anything interesting?"

"We'll never know, damn it." Grandmaw leaned back, disgusted.

Graham's cheerful expression faded.

"It's nice to see you," Andrea told him hastily. "We needed a man to even things up."

He took her remark literally. "Steve's already eaten, I guess. Darned if I know where Roger is. Do you know, Françoise?"

"*Naturellement*, he's at the shop. Where he always is . . . unless he's on a 'orse. This morning, he's getting ready to go riding with his *petite*. . . ."

"She means with me," Andrea said quietly.

"Oh." Graham was momentarily taken aback, but he rallied quickly. "Good. I'm glad to see you getting some practice, my dear. Be careful, though. Don't let Roger rush you. There's nothing he likes better than a fast gallop."

Grandmaw took a swallow of coffee. "You're behind times, Graham. A slow walk's the thing, according to Françoise."

He paused in the process of unfolding his napkin. "I don't understand. Why on earth would Roger want to walk the horses?"

Andrea cut in before Françoise could explain, "Excuse me . . . I'm late now." She got up hastily and pushed aside her chair.

"But your breakfast," Graham protested.

"I'll have coffee later, thanks."

"There's no use 'urrying." Françoise was swirling her cup languidly. "Roger'll still be at the shop . . . he's doing accounts."

"Then I'll meet him there. See you all later." Andrea picked up her flat wallet, which hooked onto the belt of her jeans, and hurried from the room. When she got

98

through the sliding doors which led out to the apron of the swimming pool, she sighed with relief. Françoise's disposition wasn't any better at the beginning of the day than the end of it. Only Steve's presence brought forth a more sympathetic nature; Graham prompted bare civility.

She struck off on the path leading past the pool down to the gift shop. Trim in jeans and an open-necked tailored white shirt, she cut an attractive figure in the morning sunshine. Her blond hair was caught back from her temples by a plain gold barrette, the ends turned under in an easy pageboy style at her collar.

Tiny gray birds were making a racket in an ocotillo bush as she walked by. They reminded her of Françoise, who seemed to cause a turmoil wherever she went. Andrea frowned as she watched the succulent's branches move under the weight of the restless flock. Surely Françoise couldn't have fooled Steve with her transparent disposition. He was logical enough about everything else. No, that wasn't quite true. Why had Roger's simple swimming invitation the night before made his face grow bleak with anger? Shaking her head thoughtfully, she moved on down the path until she came to the separate Spanish-style cottage housing the ranch gift shop.

She walked on tiptoe across the tiled porch and peered through the display window. The interior of the shop appeared deserted. Roger must be in the back storage room behind the curtained arch.

As she put her hand on the shop door, she discovered it was standing ajar. Under her fingers, it moved inward on well-oiled hinges.

Once inside the shop, Andrea heard Roger's voice in the back room, and from his one-sided remarks, deduced he was on the telephone.

She smiled faintly at the way he would break into explosive French every other sentence. As the conversation became prolonged, she decided to look around the shop area, moving quietly so that she wouldn't disturb him.

The Circle C's gift shop duplicated many others in Tucson, with the usual line of stationery, ceramic wind bells, books for children, and Indian jewelry. Comical, long-necked roadrunners were decorating everything from glassware to baby's bibs. One trip around the crowded room was enough to make Andrea decide that she didn't need to spend any of her money there.

Roger's telephone conversation went on and on. She looked at her watch and debated going down to the stable to wait for him, but the possibility of encountering Steve made her pause. He had told her to stay with the Frenchman; how would she explain any desertion?

She pushed her hands down in her tight jean pockets and moved aimlessly across the room to the desk where Roger had evidently been working before the telephone rang. There were two untidy piles of invoices scattered among the belongings in the middle of his blotter. If they hid any illegal transactions, it wasn't apparent at first glance. She took a hasty look toward the back of the shop and then leaned over to leaf through the papers. At the bottom of the far pile, she found an account sheet of a different type, which listed number combinations opposite certain dates. On an impulse, she hastily copied several of the entries on a scrap of memo paper, being careful to get the dates and numbers in proper sequence.

Then she heard the noise of the telephone receiver being replaced, and she pushed the memo in her back pocket with one hand while stuffing the invoices back into place with the other. When Roger entered the room, she was leaning against the edge of his desk.

"*Chérie!* Why didn't you tell me you were here? I meant to be finished with this before now." If he noticed her breathlessness, it wasn't apparent. "How did you know where to find me?"

"That wasn't hard. Françoise told me at breakfast." Andrea tried to edge casually away from the desk and the invoices. Roger had given the papers merely a cursory glance, but she saw that the corner of his handwritten sheet was in plain view at the bottom of the pile, where before it had been safely tucked out of sight.

"*Allons* . . . I'll do the rest of this work later," he said, dropping an account sheet he was holding on one of the stacks and then sweeping all the papers up under his arm before putting them in the drawer of a nearby file cabinet. Despite his casual manner, Andrea noted that he locked the steel drawer securely and buttoned the key in his shirt pocket. Then he turned to her, saying gaily, "I told Juan to get the horses ready. If we keep them waiting much longer, that creature of yours will be lying on his side in the sunshine even with his saddle on."

Roger kept her close beside him as they went out of the shop. He locked the door behind them and turned the cardboard sign resting against the display window from "Open" to "Closed."

"This can't be good for your business," she demurred as they went down the path toward the stables.

He shrugged, exhibiting impressive shoulder muscles under his usual tight body shirt, which was tucked into a pair of jeans. *"C'est la vie.* If you won't come swimming with me at night, then I let the customers wait in the daytime."

"And besides, you like to go riding," she told him, wrinkling her nose derisively.

"With real 'orses it would be better. These"—he gestured toward the corral—"these are for old ladies and children."

"Thanks very much."

"No need to be angry, *chérie.* I don't care for 'orsey women myself. A man doesn't invite them to go for a midnight swim." He lowered his voice suggestively. "You needn't worry today. We can go for a nice slow ride. It's easier on the horses."

Andrea recalled Françoise's words at the breakfast table and wondered if Roger was concerned solely with the horses' welfare. His solicitude didn't ring true.

"Besides," he was going on, "I need relaxation after working so hard this morning."

"You *did* have mounds of papers on your desk. I'm surprised this place is so much work."

"The shop is only a small part of it." He fished a pair of sunglasses from his pants pocket and put them on after giving the lenses a casual glance. "Most of the work comes from my family's import business. That's why I 'ave to make so many trips to Mexico . . . to make sure they keep their deliveries on schedule."

Deliveries of what, Andrea wanted to ask, feeling that he was merely returning the conversational ball to her court and not really telling her anything. Steve must have been desperate to think that the man beside her would let anything of value slip to her or any other woman.

"Can't Françoise help you?" she finally asked timidly.

"*That* one? I wish I 'ad never let my uncle send her 'ere." He glanced sideways as they crossed the gravel area in front of the corral. "*You* seem very interested in my work, Andrea. I'm flattered." Reaching out, he snaked his arm around her waist and momentarily rested his forehead against hers. "We must enjoy our time together, don't you think?"

She resisted her instinctive desire to pull away from him. Instead, she submitted to his hug docilely. "You should spread the word to Hammerhead. He's the only one giving me trouble these days."

"You're lucky." His expression darkened momentarily. "I wish I could say the same."

"What do you mean by that?" she asked with sudden hope.

He nipped her waist and then released her. "It's too nice a morning to be so serious. Ah! I see our 'orses ready and waiting." He frowned as he surveyed them. "*Dieu!* That Hammerhead should be sent to—what do you call it?—the glue factory, *n'est-ce pas?*"

Andrea's head came up quickly. "For heaven's sake, why?"

"Why? He looks like a dust bin, that's why. He's no 'orse for a lady to ride."

She was tempted to agree with him when she saw the glossy bay waiting beside her lethargic steed. Either Hammerhead had hidden virtues—very well hidden—or Steve was indulging a fiendish sense of humor.

"He's not so bad," she said halfheartedly.

Roger turned up his palms in a Gallic gesture. "We 'ave no choice this morning. There isn't time to find another one in the lower corral. Besides, Mr. York would not approve." Roger undid the reins of his mount and gathered them in one hand. "You'd think he would be 'ere working occasionally."

"Yes, you would." Andrea echoed his sentiments heartily. Steve could at least appear on the horizon now and then to boost her morale. Suppose she needed help? She chewed uneasily on the edge of her lower lip and then gave herself a mental jab. For heaven's sake, why should she need help on a morning ride?

"This must be for you." Roger removed a broad-brimmed hat from the top of a fence post near Hammerhead. Its unscathed appearance indicated the white horse didn't care for millinery as a morning snack.

"Oh . . . thanks." Andrea put it on. "I usually forget to bring one, so Juan keeps this here." As she watched Roger test his saddle cinch, she added hesitantly, "Could you give me a leg up, please?"

"Of course, *chérie*." He immediately came over to assist her. "Françoise is so self-sufficient that I forget my manners." He kept his reins in one hand as he cupped his palms. "Up you go."

Hammerhead stood stoically as Andrea scrambled into the saddle, gathering the reins into her right hand and reaching down to pat Hammerhead's neck with her left. The action raised the customary puff of dust, which hung in the still air. "Two minutes with you, and I need a bath," she told him severely. "Some noble steed you are!"

Roger had swung smoothly into the saddle, controlling his mount's gentle skittering without effort. "Shall we take the north trail?"

"Whatever you say."

He leaned toward her as he brought his horse near. "Well, it's wider . . . and I 'ave no desire to go single file this morning."

Andrea blinked. Evidently Roger was starting his campaign before they even got away from the stable. She wished fleetingly that Juan was beside her; he was always perfectly satisfied with narrow trails, and Steve . . . probably Steve would send her out alone. Only a Frenchman would try to combine *l'amour* and Hammerhead. Couldn't he see the two didn't mix? She gathered the reins more tightly in her hand and gave him a brilliant smile. "The north trail sounds fine. You can watch me show off."

"What is this?"

"Juan's been telling me how to make Hammerhead move. So far I've worked on the trot and the canter. Now let's try his gallop." She dug her heels into the horse's well-upholstered middle as she spoke. Startled, Hammerhead responded as if he'd been summoned by Matt Dillon himself.

When they returned an hour and a half later, it was hard to tell which member of the party was the more disgruntled. Hammerhead hung his head, looking thoroughly maligned. An onlooker would have thought he'd been forced to cross Death Valley in a time trial. His sides heaved, his tail swished, and his ears were plastered back in annoyance.

Roger was sulking almost as obviously. Each time that he's suggested stopping during the ride, Andrea had found something of interest an acre away and was off again. He'd heard about the energy of American women—now he knew what it meant. All he'd gotten out of the morning was a view of her disappearing shoulder blades and a headache from the heat. He cast her a surreptitious look as they moved up to the corral gate. She was slumping in the saddle despite her attempts to ignore fatigue. While he watched, a rivulet of perspiration dropped down her flushed cheek, and it was an obvious effort for her to rub it away. His lips curved in a slow smile. Next time she'd know better than to try to escape from a man.

He would have been surprised to learn that her thoughts were running on the same track. Nothing, Andrea decided, absolutely nothing was worth the effort she'd exerted to keep Roger at arm's length—or horse's width—during that miserable ride. At the moment, she was wondering how she'd dismount from Hammerhead without sinking onto the ground under his hooves. If that happened, the only thing that would save her was the fact that he was probably too tired to do anything about it.

Even then, he couldn't be as tired as she was. Her arm muscles ached, her back muscles ached, and her legs felt like two pieces of spaghetti as they hugged Hammerhead's girth. And if Roger didn't stop leering at her as he had on the entire ride, she'd hit him over the head with a bootjack when they got back in the stable. If she had the strength to lift it.

"You'll need to cool off after such a fast ride. What about a jump in the swimming pool," Roger asked as he watched her pull to a stop.

Andrea hung onto the saddlehorn grimly when she slithered down Hammerhead's side. The horse didn't even bother to look around as she rested her forehead for a split-second against him and fought for a deep breath. "That sounds like a good idea," she said finally, trying for a light tone, "but what do we do with our horses? Shouldn't they be rubbed down?"

"Don't worry about that." Drops of perspiration coated

Roger's forehead as he pulled his own horse up and dismounted. Grabbing Hammerhead's reins from her, he added impatiently, "I'll take care of them."

"But you shouldn't have to bother with that. . . ."

"I don't plan to. One of the 'ands will do the work. He's coming now." He nodded toward the lower pasture, where a man carrying a pitchfork over his shoulder was moving toward the stable.

"Oh, I hadn't realized." Her words trailed off.

"You worry too much, Andrea. It's a bad 'abit . . . being too anxious." His dark eyes were enigmatic as his glance flicked over her flushed face. "Go on up and cool off. I'll see you at lunch."

"All right, Roger." She was too tired to discuss it further. As she went by the fence, she took off her hat and hung it on a convenient post, where it hung limply, looking exactly the way she felt.

Her walk to the main ranch buildings made her acknowledge that Roger's suggestion regarding a swim was a good one. For one thing, it postponed the final trudge up the hill to her cottage under the searing midday sun. Françoise and a few of the other guests were lazily disporting themselves in the outdoor pool, so Andrea veered off on the path leading to the indoor pool down the hill. She was thankful for the shade trees bordering the narrow walk, and once she stepped inside the stucco building housing the athletic facilities, the breeze from the air-conditioner felt so good that she could have sat down on the tile floor and offered thanks to the gods. Instead, she took a deep breath and walked on to the women's dressing room, where spare swimsuits were kept for the guests. She picked out a two-piece blue nylon in her size and started to peel off her riding clothes. Shedding the jeans was pure bliss, the long-sleeved shirt almost as good. By the time she was clad in the brief swimsuit, she felt that she might be able to survive until lunchtime. Never, never again would she ride pell-mell through the desert heat. If Roger suggested another date—which was doubtful—it would have to be on air-conditioned premises. And if Steve were unhappy about this morning, he'd just have to design another plan of attack.

Her eyes clouded when she considered that. It would have been wonderful if she could have reported some startling developments. Instead, all she could truthfully say was that their prime suspect was convinced that any woman should be eager to fall into his arms—even on horseback. Thank heaven Hammerhead hadn't been any happier about that idea than she had.

She selected a towel from a stack in the corner and padded out into the hall, before pausing and wondering what to do first. Grandmaw Carter had been extolling the virtues of the sauna bath, followed by the therapy pool, followed by the exercise room, followed by ten minutes in the big indoor pool. Andrea shook her head as she considered the program. If she did all that, it would be followed by her complete collapse. Five minutes in the Finnish bath, she decided, then a refreshing swim in the pool. She turned down the hall to the door marked "Sauna."

The intense heat made her gasp as she entered the deserted room and groped her way to a wooden bench. As she stretched out, she kept her glance on the big clock above the stone-covered heating element. Five minutes would definitely be long enough, she decided.

The sweep second hand had no sooner hit the twelve on the clock face, indicating passage of the required interval, than she was on her feet ready to leave the room. Any more of that concentrated heat and she would have been trying for a second case of heat prostration.

The latch moved upward under her fingers, but the door stuck stubbornly in the frame. Damn, she thought grimly —this was all she needed. She took a firmer grip on the latch and heaved upward.

The door remained stubbornly in place.

Sudden, unreasoning panic hit her stomach muscles as her subconscious registered the hiss of hot air blanketing the room behind her. The big glass thermometer showed a marking of 190 degrees, and her imagination took flight. Even ten more minutes in here and she'd be too weak to cry out.

She dropped the latch and reached up frantically to pound on the middle of the door. "Let me out of here . . . oh, please . . . help me."

The silence that followed her cries was eerie. Only the serpentlike sizzle continued to come from the heater in the corner.

Andrea made herself pull away from the door and move over to it. If she could find the thermostat, she wouldn't have to worry. Desperately she searched around the stone-covered pyramid.

Nothing!

Her hopes collapsed like a punctured balloon when she realized the control must be mounted outside the room.

Wraithlike, she moved back to the door, feeling that just being close to the hallway offered a shade of protection from the stifling heat. She blotted her wet palms on the sides of her swim trunks before reaching for the metal latch again. When the door remained firmly closed despite her efforts, she moaned softly and let her forehead fall against its hot surface . . . too discouraged to cry out or pound any longer.

Chapter EIGHT

When the door to the sauna was finally opened, Andrea had collapsed into a limp heap on the floor next to it.

"Oh, my Gawd!" Grandmaw Carter shrieked. "What's wrong with you, girl?"

In Andrea's bemused state, she couldn't manage a coherent answer just then. All she knew was that the gates of heaven wouldn't have looked more welcome than that open door with the cool air rushing through it.

"Let's get you out of here," Grandmaw was murmuring next to her ear. "Hang onto me—there's a padded bench in the next room. Can you manage, dear?" Tenderness vied with urgency in her voice.

This time Andrea was able to nod faintly, and with Grandmaw's surprisingly strong arm around her waist, pulled herself erect and stumbled out of the room.

The next thing she knew, she was being pushed gently onto a foam-rubber-padded bench, with Grandmaw saying, "Lie right there ... I'll go and get help."

"No ... I'm all right. Just let me rest a few minutes. Oh, please"—Andrea pushed herself up on an elbow—"I don't need anyone but you."

"An old lady's no good for something like this," Grandmaw said, chin quivering with determination. She pulled a toweling robe from a nearby hook and wrapped it around her swimsuit. "You need a man. We both do. And I want to find out why that sliver of wood was wedged in the door latch."

"Don't call Graham," Andrea wailed, knowing she was being unreasonable but unable to control the tears that welled in her eyes. "Let me just stay here quietly for a few minutes ... with the door open. I'm sorry to be so silly but I ... I ... can't help it."

Grandmaw frowned and then bent down to pat her comfortingly on the shoulder. "Ssh, girl. Don't fuss. That's delayed shock causing your waterworks. Perfectly normal after a fright like that. Lord almighty—you could have been killed in that hotbox."

"I know," Andrea sniffed, and wiped her cheek with the back of her hand. "Oh, God, I know."

"Well, it's over now, and I don't think you're much the worse for wear. . . ." Grandmaw rose and stepped protectively in front of Andrea as they heard the outer door open. "Who is it?" she called out in her normal rasp. "We don't want company right now."

The footsteps in the tiled hallway paused, and then Steve stuck his head around the archway, frowning. His swift glance took in the older woman's defensive stance and Andrea's pale face. "What the devil's going on?" he growled.

Grandmaw collapsed on the end of the bench beside Andrea. "Steve . . . thank the lord. You're the very one I wanted to see!"

He'd moved over in front of Andrea's slumped figure and grasped her wrist, counting the pulse as he stood there with a grim look on his face. "What happened, Mrs. Carter?"

"I'm all right. . . ." Andrea tried to pull her hand away, but he held it in an iron grip. "I just got locked in the sauna."

"*You* keep quiet!" His glance passed over her face, and he bent down to feel her forehead with his other hand. "How about a cold towel before the explanation, Mrs. Carter?"

"I'll get it right away." She moved quickly out into the hall.

Steve continued to stare down at Andrea while they waited for her return. "Why?" he asked finally. "Why, why, why?"

His lack of inflection chilled her almost as much as the cold towel which Grandmaw put into her hands a minute later. Andrea pressed the folded pad of terry to her temples and the side of her neck before saying helplessly, "I don't know . . . I thought it was an accident."

"Accident, my foot!" Grandmaw rasped. "There was a sliver of wood wedging that lock, I tell you. If I hadn't changed my mind about taking a sauna bath before lunch, this poor girl could still be frying in that place."

"Well, thank heaven I'm not," the "poor girl" replied, sitting up straighter as the horror began to pass off. "And I'm all right," she repeated, "honestly I am."

"Then you can stay here by yourself while I take a look at that door," Steve told her. "Mrs. Carter, can you show me that piece of wood?"

"You bet . . . just follow me."

Andrea watched them turn down the hallway before she leaned against the wall behind her. She closed her eyes and consciously made her mind go blank while willing her muscles to relax.

Steve found her in that position when he came back. "I'll take you up to your cottage now if you're able."

Her eyes flew open. "Of course." She stood up, still clutching the cold towel. "Where's Mrs. Carter?"

"She went back to her room. Said she was all out of the mood for this place right now." His slanted smile appeared briefly. "She only left after I promised to see you safely home."

"There was no need for that," Andrea began.

"Don't be a fool. C'mon, I have the jeep outside."

"But my clothes . . . they're still in the dressing room."

"Then I'll pick them up so you can take them along," he said resignedly.

"I can't go jeep riding in this outfit," she protested, indicating the brief swimsuit.

"Why not? You could make three bikinis out of it and have material left over. Besides, all I'm doing is taking you home in the middle of the day—not scheduling an orgy."

"All right, but you have to promise to wait in the dressing-room doorway while I collect my things."

"Exactly what I had in mind."

It was on the ride up to her cottage that Andrea turned to him. "Did you warn Mrs. Carter about mentioning this trouble?"

His mouth clamped into a stern line, and he turned into the parking space behind her cottage before answering. "I asked her to keep quiet," he said tersely. "Want me to carry those clothes for you?"

"No thanks, I can manage them." She bundled them under her arm as she opened the door.

"Sit still until I get around there," he ordered. "If you

110

try to walk on the gravel around this place with bare feet, you'll really be in bad shape."

"Maybe you're right." Her voice was hesitant as she peered over the side of the jeep.

"Raise the flag—the woman's agreeing with me." He came around to her side and bent down to lift her in his arms. "All you have to do is close the door."

Andrea tried to breathe naturally as they went around the side of the cottage. A skimpy swimsuit couldn't hide the fact that the accelerated thump of her heart could be heard in the next county. Either that, or Steve's was pounding faster than usual. Surely she wasn't *that* heavy. She glanced up, and then quickly lowered her eyes as her curious gaze met his brooding one.

"The key," she said in some confusion, "it's in my jeans pocket. You can put me down on the porch while I get it. I can walk now," she added unnecessarily as he pulled up at the front door.

He lowered her feet to the cement porch without saying anything. She moved a few inches away from his tall frame and made a production out of finding her key. "Here it is," she said, waving it triumphantly but still avoiding his gaze. "Thanks very much for bringing me here. . . ."

He reached out and plucked it from her fingers. "I'm coming in." Unlocking the door, he gestured her ahead of him.

Andrea stood in the center of the bedroom, clutching her riding things protectively. "There's nothing wrong with me this time," she asserted nervously. "Frankly, I was just scared to death at the thought of being parboiled in that place."

Steve was still lounging against the closed door, his hands shoved in his pockets. "Get some clothes on, Andy," he said impassively.

Her eyes widened in surprise. "I intend to . . . when you've gone. And I wish you'd stop calling me by that horrible nickname."

"Sorry." He started prowling around the room. "Throw something on now. I want to talk to you, and the way you're dressed"—his eyes raked her slim form deliberately —"you make it difficult for a man to keep his mind on his work. Hurry up . . . I can't stay here alone with you very long."

"You mean somebody's watching?" she asked, turning obediently toward the dressing room. Under the circumstances, it seemed safer to ignore his other comment.

"Is that so surprising, after what happened to you already today?"

She stopped rummaging through the hangers in her closet to peer over her shoulder. "Then you agree with Grandmaw Carter that it was deliberate?"

"I'd say a deliberate attempt to frighten you . . . nothing more." He watched her pull on a full-length ivory shantung robe over the swimsuit. As she stepped into a pair of matching slippers, he added, "If they'd really wanted to harm you, it was the hard way to go about it."

She raked her hair back and went into the bedroom, tying her belt as she walked. "How can you say that?"

"Because Françoise had a conditioning class scheduled in the exercise room in twenty minutes. A stop-off in the sauna is part of her daily regime. The place would have been crawling with people, but that doesn't minimize your experience. You'd better sit down and rest for a while."

Since Andrea felt distinctly light-headed, she wasn't disposed to argue with him. She looked at the bed and then gave it a wide berth to sit in the upholstered chair by the desk.

If Steve noticed her nervousness, he was kind enough to ignore it. He went over to sit on the end of the bed and leaned toward her, his elbows on his knees. "Exactly what happened on the ride this morning?"

"Nothing . . . not a darned thing." She couldn't hide the bitterness in her voice. "No thanks to that wolf of a Frenchman, though. The only thing on his mind was . . ." Her words trailed off in embarrassment.

Steve's lips thinned. "I get the idea."

"So did he . . . finally. But only after I'd kept Hammerhead flat out for the whole ride."

"That's an accomplishment in itself." Steve scraped his thumb along his jaw thoughtfully. "Then you did nothing to make Roger suspicious or angry rather than use evasive tactics?"

"I don't think so. Unless . . ."—she frowned—"unless he could have seen me looking over his desk."

Steve's head came up abruptly. "When was that?"

"Earlier." Andrea explained how she'd waited in the gift shop during the telephone conversation. She finished by saying, "He couldn't have known that I'd been through the invoices unless he saw the corner of that list." Her frown deepened. "But he wouldn't have cared even then unless it was something important. Damn! I suppose I'll never know." She started to shrug and broke off, grimacing with sudden pain.

Steve stood up abruptly, his eyes narrowing. "You're in worse shape than I realized. I'll call the doctor."

"For heaven's sake, no! It's just a crick in my shoulder. I probably got it when I was yanking at that darned sauna door. Sit down . . . you make it worse when you tower over me."

He sat down, but on the arm of her chair this time. "Lean forward . . . maybe I can massage it out." Before she could protest, his hands started to knead the nape of her neck. "Is this the place?"

"A little more to the left," she acknowledged, wondering if she should tell him that the warmth of those strong hands through the thin material of her robe wasn't relaxing. Just the opposite.

He must have received the unspoken message. His thumbs stopped their gentle circular motion along her collarbone. "You're as tight as a bow string . . . loosen up, can't you? Let your head fall forward. That's it." With a sudden movement, he pulled the robe back from her shoulders. "It's in the way," he explained, ignoring her gasp. "There—that's better." His hands feathered along the shoulder for some minutes. Since he merely worked over the strap of her swimsuit, she kept meekly silent.

Steve focused his glance on the back of her bent head. "I think you'd better keep out of Roger's way for the next day or so."

"He didn't seem suspicious." Andrea wasn't convinced. "You could be on the wrong track."

"You must have been getting too close to something," he insisted. "Damned if I can figure out what it was. Tell me again what that list looked like."

"Dates on the left, and columns of numbers on the right."

"Any dollar signs or notations to indicate currency?"

She shook her head. "Nothing. It's a pity you couldn't have searched that file-cabinet drawer."

"By now, five would get you ten that we'd find it empty. Roger's worked in the family 'businesses' long enough to avoid leaving anything around." He broke off as she gave a sudden start. "What's the matter? Did I rub too hard?"

"No, it's not that." She swiveled in the chair to face him. "I think I *am* losing my mind—I'd forgotten that I copied a little bit of that list. If you'll wait a second, I'll get it from my jeans, unless . . ."

"Unless somebody decided to go through your pockets after disposing of you in the sauna. Go take a look," he instructed tersely.

She came back from the dressing room waving the slip of paper triumphantly. "Let's have an extra ration for the troops, *mon général*. They didn't take it, after all! I didn't *think* Roger was very suspicious."

"I should beat you for taking a chance like that," Steve groused as he reached for the paper.

"Oh, come on . . . stop being so cross and tell me if it's any help."

His eyebrows drew together in concentration as he read the few lines she had scribbled. "I'll be damned," he said eventually.

"That doesn't tell me very much."

He ignored her frivolity and folded the paper carefully before buttoning it into his shirt pocket. "I don't know very much yet, but at least you've given me a couple of new ideas. Let's wait and see."

"Then you think Roger was the one who jammed that door?" she persisted.

"It points that way, or he could have enlisted Françoise's help. There was plenty of time. It's immaterial. From now on, stick close to friendly faces in the daytime. Tonight, Juan and I'll keep an eye on this cottage. Tomorrow, the trip to Nogales is on . . . and after that . . ."

"What then?"

"Then you check out and spend the rest of your holiday in Coronado or La Jolla."

"Oh." She digested those laconic words and found they

114

didn't go down well at all. "I haven't been what you'd call a resounding success at this, have I?"

At her timid query, Steve put out a cautious finger to touch a strand of soft blond hair, and then pulled back abruptly.

She gazed up at him solemnly. "What's the matter?"

"Nothing. I have to get going. Remember to take it easy for the rest of the day."

"All right." She matched his terseness, although his sudden change of mood bewildered her. From the way he spoke, she was right back in the doubtful category—like the day they'd met. He must be regretting the fact that he'd ever enlisted her help.

He strode over to the door. "Grandmaw Carter will come up and keep you company for lunch. I've asked her to keep her eyes open. Later on, how about doing some leisurely shopping in town?"

"Do you think that might cheer her up? I know she's unhappy since Ellie's gone."

"It won't hurt. You can do each other a good turn."

"Well, if you say so." Andrea still sounded doubtful. "When do we go to Mexico? Tomorrow?"

"Late afternoon, the way things are now. We should be back before midnight." He paused with his hand on the doorknob. "It has to look like a casual date," he warned. "The places we'll be going aren't on the American Express tour list."

"You treat me as if I'm six years old," she complained, pulling the sash of her robe tighter as she frowned at him. "Just because I didn't let Roger be . . . obnoxious . . . this morning doesn't mean that I'm a fragile 'little woman.' "

He smiled slightly. "You're tough, and you can take care of yourself. Is that it?"

"Well . . ." she wavered, remembering the temperature of that sauna, ". . . most of the time."

"Okay." He became businesslike again. "There shouldn't be any problems in Nogales. You're strictly window dressing. Incidentally, if you can wear something sort of . . ." He gestured graphically.

"Form-fitting?" Her eyebrows drew together. "I suppose so. What's the idea?"

"Nogales is a border town, and this isn't a dancing-

115

school date, so leave your white gloves at home. I want the natives to look at you and keep right on looking. Anything tight and bright will be fine. Wear plenty of makeup and perfume."

"Good Lord, you make me sound like a doxy," she got out faintly. "Do I have to lean against a light post, too?"

"That isn't on the schedule. Juan or I will be with you all the time, so you don't have to worry about your virtue. The Mexicans are enthusiastic, but they're realistic." He rubbed the top of his nose reflectively. "All I want you to do is look like a flashy, not very bright tourist. You talk too loud, wriggle your hips when you walk, and come home with an armful of piñatas. Understand?"

She swallowed. "I guess so. I'll buy something to wear this afternoon."

He had the door halfway open. "Keep track of your expenses . . . the department will reimburse you."

She started to laugh.

"Now what?" He hovered in the doorway, patently impatient to be gone.

"Nothing." She shook her head helplessly. "I always wondered how it felt to be a kept woman. . . ."

He grinned. "Now you'll know. Uncle Sugar pays the bill. Remember, tight and bright—the kind your mother wouldn't approve of."

"I get the message." She bit her lip. "Let's hope that Roger doesn't see me in it when I leave."

"Don't worry. You can wear your coat until we get to the border." The door closed behind him.

It was after dinner the next day when they finally got under way.

Andrea was sandwiched on the front seat of her car between Steve and Juan's considerable bulk. "I could sit in the back," she protested feebly. "This makes it an awful squeeze for you."

Juan, who was driving, gave her an undisturbed glance. "Doesn't bother me. How about you, Steve?"

"Plenty of room . . . now," the latter said, shifting slightly in the seat and draping his arm along the top of it. He looked down at Andrea. "You'd be more comfortable if you took off that coat."

"Nuh-uh." She shook her head emphatically.

"Aren't you warm . . . all buttoned up like that?"

She started to laugh. "Not in the least. Once you see my outfit, you'll understand why. Grandmaw thought I was losing my mind when I bought it yesterday. She said even Ellie would have had more sense."

"Sounds great to me," Juan said, grinning.

Andrea noticed Steve's lack of response. "You needn't look so disapproving," she informed him. "It was your idea, after all. Don't tell me you've changed your mind?"

"I'd like to," he admitted, "but we need you more than ever now. We got the word late this afternoon that Eric's in Nogales and finally ready to talk."

"Then the end's in sight. . . ."

"Don't count on it. Plenty can happen before we get to Eric. Once he turns informer, his life isn't worth a damn."

"But why Mexico? Why doesn't he come back to Tucson?"

"Because he's waiting for our payoff before he splits. Those are his words . . . precisely. He thinks he can lose himself easier south of the border than he can up here. At this point, he's buying time."

"I can't understand why that bothers you," she said, frowning. "Granted, he's only eighteen, but that's old enough to make his own decisions, and they couldn't even change his mind at the hospital."

"Eric isn't the one who's bothering me," Steve said abruptly. "Ellie was seen in Nogales with him yesterday. The way he's going, it's strictly a one-way street. There's no future for a girl friend."

"But that's terrible . . . you'll have to tell her."

"We'll try," Juan spoke up grimly, "if we can get close enough. I'll drag her across the border personally."

"Does her grandmother know?"

"Not yet," Steve said. "We just heard ourselves this afternoon. An official inquiry won't accomplish anything. Those kids know how to hide, and a Mexican border town makes it easier than usual."

"I hope Eric's looking after her. . . ."

"An addict!" Juan braked for a stop sign so hard that she had to brace herself against the dashboard. "You don't know much about the drug racket, Andrea. Eric can only exert one kind of influence at this point—and it's all bad. Ellie's fool enough to think she can change him."

"It's been done."

117

"Only when the addict makes up his own mind first. Eric hasn't. He's turning informer to keep himself supplied. If he wanted help, he merely has to come back to the hospital in Tucson."

"Let's forget it for a while." Steve's voice was heavy. "There's no use anticipating trouble."

"How long will it take to reach Nogales?" Andrea asked for a diversion.

He shrugged. " 'Round an hour and a half. We've plenty of time to make our appointment." He went on in tones of polite inquiry. "Any trouble after that business yesterday?"

"If you mean the stiff neck"—she shook her head—"it's gone, thanks. Grandmaw was by my side all afternoon, and I gather that everything was quiet during the night." She made it a statement of fact rather than a question. When he nodded negligently, she went on, "When do you get any sleep?"

Juan broke in. "We don't . . . not enough. Right now I could hibernate for a week."

Steve spoke up mildly. "Maybe I should be driving." He grinned at Juan's prompt derisive gesture and then glanced back at Andrea. "The first time I met you, you were convinced that I spent my time lolling around; now you're worried about my health. I'm glad that virtue finally triumphed."

She made a rude noise. "My first opinion hasn't changed that much."

"Then we'll have to work on it." Blandly he continued, "How did you keep occupied today?"

"Eating . . . napping . . . sunning." Her lips quirked. "Staying at the shallow end of the pool. Françoise has officially washed her hands of me."

"No hope for the underdeveloped shoulder muscles?"

So he'd remembered. Andrea felt a tiny glow. "None at all. She's concentrating on a manufacturer from New Jersey who has splendid biceps. Maybe you've noticed," she added impishly.

"Maybe." He wasn't about to be drawn. "Grandmaw said you spent a lot of time in the lounge."

She flushed slightly. "You *do* have a good spy system. Was it really necessary?"

"After yesterday . . . what do you think?"

"That I'd better apologize," she granted, mollified. "Did Grandmaw also report that I spent considerable time with Graham?"

"I'm asking you," he reminded her. "Still on your archaeology kick?"

She nodded. "It's perfectly fascinating. He found me reading some of the books in the lounge and told me about a lot more reference material. I'd love to go out on one of their weekend outings." She peeped sideways under half-lowered lashes. "If I could get the extra vacation time, maybe I could hang around a little longer?"

Steve's jaw firmed. "We've been through that. You leave tomorrow. Preferably still in one piece," he added forcefully.

Even in the limited space, she managed to flounce angrily on the seat. "I shouldn't have asked you."

"That's right, you shouldn't."

"Although I don't know why I can't stay if I want to. It's still a free country, and I'm over twenty-one." She could see Juan's shoulders shaking with laughter, but a glance on the other side revealed that Steve wasn't amused.

"I'll put it this way," he said evenly. "You go . . . willingly or unwillingly. You can walk on the airplane or I'll carry you on kicking. Besides, Graham already has a reservation for your cottage this weekend." He glanced at her rebellious face and nodded. "That's right, I made it myself. There's no room at the inn, little one. Send me an address when you get settled, and we'll give you a follow-up on what happened." He turned to stare out the side window, effectively stopping the discussion.

There was an awkward silence, which no one made any effort to fill until Juan cleared his throat and said, "We'll pass Tumacacori Monument on this road, Andrea. If you're interested in old stuff, you'll get a kick out of seeing what's left of the chapel when we drive by."

Since he was trying so obviously to make amends for Steve's curtness, Andrea decided to help him. As for the silent creature on her right, he'd find out eventually that he couldn't pawn off any woman quite so easily.

They reached the border town of Nogales, Arizona, just at twilight.

Andrea looked across at Juan in surprise when he

119

parked the car a block from the modern International Bridge marking the border. "Why are we stopping on the American side?" she asked.

"It's easier," Steve replied. "We can move out fast if we have to." From his unruffled air, one would never have known that he was issuing ultimatums to her an hour before.

Well, *he* might have forgotten, Andrea decided, but she hadn't. Still, she could bide her time. Obediently, she got out of the car as he held the door. "You mean we walk?" she asked.

"Got it in one," he said with gentle sarcasm.

She pressed her lips together to keep from arguing. As he just stood there beside the car, she asked querulously, "What are we waiting for?"

"The coat. You'll have to shed it sometime. Now's as good as any." The lines around his mouth deepened with amusement.

"Oh!" Andrea began to unbutton her coat slowly. She finally handed it over like a French prisoner relinquishing his most cherished possession before mounting the steps to the guillotine.

Juan took one look at her, grinned widely, and then turned to toss her coat in the car before he locked the doors. Steve, if possible, looked grimmer than ever.

Andrea scowled in response. *Now* what had she done? He'd said tight and bright, hadn't he? Well, they didn't come much brighter than the sleazy scarlet-and-white print dress she was wearing. Parts of it were sticking to her like kitchen cement. Of course, there was a considerable draft in other parts. . . .

Despite his stolid mien, Steve was agreeing with her. After one look at that miniskirted dress, he felt like bundling her straight back to Tucson. The night promised to be rough enough without a woman walking the streets of a border town garbed like that. His glance flicked over the dress again. The demure collar was offset by a zipper running all the way down the center of the bodice to the hipline, and the zipper pull was big enough for a Ubangi nose ring. Fortunately, the zipper was closed . . . and it had better stay that way, he decided, because the damned dress was backless to the waist. There was some sort of a belt at the hipline—although that was a waste of time, because there wasn't enough spare material to need belting. Only a scant six inches of pleated skirt ending at mid-thigh.

Steve took a deep breath and let it out.

Andrea heard him. "Is it . . . all right?" she asked meekly, glad that the high collar of the dress hid the blush which had started from her ankles and moved upward.

"Fine. Just fine," Steve said hollowly.

Juan had difficulty remaining serious. "Great," he confirmed.

"We'll make sure not to leave you alone," Steve said, moving to her side. "You can walk between us." He caught her elbow and maneuvered her into place. "Now, stay there."

She pulled her arm away. "Try to remember that I only have two legs . . . not four," she said sweetly. "I bruise easier than Hammerhead."

"I'll remember," he told her grimly. "On you . . . the marks would show." His glance swept over her. "Practically everywhere. You say Grandmaw was along when you bought the dress?"

She nodded. "It was all right, though. I didn't need a permission slip."

This time she watched with enjoyment as *his* neck turned red.

"Come on . . . let's get moving," he muttered. He gave her a sideways glance as they started down the sidewalk toward the boundary gate. "After tonight, you can donate it to a gypsy rummage sale. It should go over big there."

"I think I'll keep it and get my ears pierced instead," she told him. "The style grows on you."

"I hope so," he said balefully. "The skirt could stand about six more inches."

Juan, who had been listening to their exchange with amusement, suddenly pulled up in the middle of the sidewalk. "Take it easy, you two. The way you're going, it can only lead to bloodshed. The dress is okay, Steve . . . you know it is. Besides," he added placatingly, "it'll be dark in twenty minutes."

"You're right," Steve admitted. "Okay, Andrea . . . I apologize."

"That's all right." She looked sheepish. "If you want the truth, I can't stand the thing . . . that's why I wore

121

my coat all the way down." She shivered suddenly. "I'm all goosebumps. Do you suppose it's nerves, or the ventilation in this dress?"

"There's only one way to find out." Steve caught her arm, companionably this time. "We'll walk fast and stir up your circulation."

Andrea's first impression of the Mexican city of Nogales wasn't enthusiastic. She turned to look at the border fence behind them and then peered up at her escorts. "Is this the *good* part of town?"

"I don't think there is one," Juan said, steering her carefully away from two lounging youths who were taking up most of the sidewalk.

Her face fell. "You mean it's all curio shops . . . block after block of it?"

"Hardly. Take another look," Steve said. "Between every curio shop there's a liquor store; where there isn't a liquor store, there's a bar. Very high-class joint."

She glanced over her shoulder. "I hope the president of the Chamber of Commerce isn't walking behind us."

"There's so much noise that he couldn't hear, anyway," Juan said, bending down to her ear. "My ancestors are certainly festive people."

Andrea decided he had a point. Soulful mariachi music spilled out of the crowded curio shops onto the sidewalks. Inside, the shopkeepers shouted happily at their employees, the customers, or anyone else who happened within earshot. Each liquor store they passed resounded with the noise of clinking glass, and jukeboxes blasted in the bars. As dusk fell, the neon signs painted a tableau of garish pictures in the sky. Lampposts were so few and far between that the light which fell on the sidewalk was mainly multicolored from signs in the shop windows.

The throng on the sidewalk became thicker. The shoppers were mainly American tourists, but the loungers propping up the buildings were Mexicans who found their enjoyment in watching the strangers. Cars careened through the narrow streets, narrowly avoiding jaywalking pedestrians with a screech of brakes. Occasionally a local bus would lurch by, emitting a cloud of exhaust.

Andrea shook her head.

"What's the matter?" asked Steve, who was watching her.

"I was just thinking that ecologists could have a field day with their local transportation." She shook her head at a sidewalk salesman who was offering "Bracelets . . . verry cheap, lady."

"How long do we go on with the city tour?" she asked finally, when they had wandered past six blocks of shops.

"Not much longer," Steve said. He steered her around the corner into a dimly lighted side street. "You and Juan are going to wait in a bar here while I try to contact Eric."

"You mean *that* place?" Andrea indicated a sagging frame building with a sign reading "Tres Ojos" propped over the open door. Two disreputable men lounged in the doorway, one cleaning his fingernails with a wicked-looking knife.

"That's the place." Steve kept his voice low. "Here's where you go into your act. Find a table in there and order a couple of beers." He smoothed the back of her collar with one hand. "Remember, this is your kind of place."

Andrea turned to Juan. "Shouldn't you be with Steve? I can manage to wait in a bar alone."

"Follow orders, damn it!" Steve snapped. He looked at Juan. "You know what to do. I should be back in fifteen minutes. See you later." He left them abruptly, cutting across the shadowed street and disappearing between two buildings.

Juan marched her across to the open doorway of the bar and then through the small crowded room to a round table near the wall. "Wait here," he ordered. "I'll get the beer."

She sat down uneasily on a bentwood chair that felt as if the grime of the ages were on it. Conversation had died down while the patrons had watched their entrance, but now it was picking up again. Andrea looked around the room casually, trying to appear natural. The jukebox beside her was missing a section of its innards, she noted gratefully; that must be why there was an undernourished guitarist perched on a stool in the corner. He was strumming chords and appearing profoundly bored with life. Her glance moved on to the dark-paneled bar. With two old-fashioned light fixtures on the wavy mirror behind rows of bottles, and Wyatt Earp waving his pistols, it could have been Dodge City instead of Nogales. Only the signs

123

reading "Cerveza" and "Bebe Coca Cola" hanging on the paneling along with the picture of a highly overdeveloped but underdressed señorita added the Mexican touch. A velvet hanging showing three prominent eyeballs was tacked over the door. Andrea averted her own eyes hastily.

"Here you are, honey." Juan dumped two bottles of beer on the table and pulled up a chair close to her. "Now we snuggle up and forget the rest of the world."

She managed to smile. "I'd love to . . . especially this particular part of it." She kept the smile pasted on as she leaned over the table toward him. "What do we do . . . drink out of the bottle?"

He nodded and handed her one of them. "I watched the bartender washing glasses . . . it's better this way."

She shuddered.

"Relax and look on the bright side. The beer's good." He took a long swallow of it. "Too bad Steve couldn't have dropped in here first."

"You're right . . . it *is* good," she said in some surprise. Then, "How long do we have to stay here?"

"That depends. Steve said fifteen minutes." A frown creased his forehead. "I think he was being optimistic."

"Was he going to pay off Eric tonight?"

"That's the general idea." He looked around casually. "Better keep your voice down."

"Oh, I'm sorry." Her gaze dropped to the table. "Are we attracting attention?"

"*You* are." His glance went idly around the room. "That outfit of yours is working out just fine . . . the guitarist is all thumbs."

"Now I know how the tethered goat feels in a tiger hunt."

"You won't get hurt. . . ."

She shook her head. "I didn't mean that. Isn't Steve taking an awful chance carrying all that money?" She saw by the way his jaw hardened that her fears weren't imagined. "I wish you'd follow him. There's certainly safety in numbers, and I won't stir out of this place."

"Sorry. Steve gives the orders, I obey them." His expression softened. "Don't worry . . . he's damned good at taking care of himself."

"But the Mexican authorities don't know you're doing this, do they?"

"Informers don't cooperate when you call in a regiment of policemen," Juan said wryly. "The less fuss, the better . . . just bring money, and then get the hell out of there."

Andrea's hand trembled on the tabletop. Hastily she dropped it in her lap, but not before Juan had seen the telltale movement.

"Steve's right—you shouldn't have been dragged into this," he started to say, and then broke off as he shot to his feet. "Ellie! I'll be damned! What's she doing here?"

Andrea spun in her chair as he pushed through the crowded tables to the girl standing dazedly in the doorway. It was hard to recognize her as the same person who'd been at the Circle C. Her eyes were circled with weariness, the long hair that had gleamed softly about her face was unkempt and straggly, adding years to her age. Her jeans were wrinkled, and her grimy orange sweater merely emphasized her thinness. As Juan bent over her near the door, her shoulders heaved with silent sobs. Conversation in the room subsided to low murmurs as every man in the place watched the couple eagerly.

Finally Juan made a sharp exclamation and came striding back to Andrea's table. Ellie was left staring dismally at the floor while trying to wipe away her tears with the back of a dirty hand.

Juan bent over Andrea's shoulder. "Something's gone wrong," he said in a low, strained voice. "Steve sent word to get her across the border . . . fast. Let's go!"

"But what about Eric?"

"Somebody took care of him before Steve reached him. From what Ellie says, the kid went out with an overdose." He glanced quickly over his shoulder. "Come on . . . I'll meet Steve here after I get you two over the border."

She shook her head firmly. "No deal . . . I'm staying here."

"Andrea, I haven't got time to argue."

"Then don't. Go ahead with Ellie," she told him just as tersely. "I'll wait here for Steve . . . right here . . . so there's no need to worry." Her hands were clenched in a tight ball in her lap. "Oh, go *on*, Juan. Don't you see . . . I have to stay."

The anguish in her voice and her unhappy face convinced him. He nodded briefly, said, "I'll be back as soon as I can," and strode back to the door. Flinging a protective arm around Ellie's shoulders, he led her out into the night.

The bar's customers avidly watched the departure, and then, as one, swung their gaze back to Andrea.

Their expressions made her flush and look away in confusion. Oh, lord, she thought dismally, now I know how the "other woman" feels. The patrons had apparently decided that she needed someone to replace Juan, and the two seedy creatures at the next table were about to volunteer. *Then* what would she do? No wonder Steve hadn't wanted to leave her alone in the place!

If there were a policeman . . . but there wasn't even a telephone to call one, and besides, you couldn't call a policeman like a taxi. She shook her head ruefully. The only thing that would work was a full-fledged riot. And if that greasy-looking Casanova at the next table moved his chair any closer, she might just start one. She took a firm grip on her bottle of beer.

The guitarist in the corner dutifully began a thready arrangement of "La Paloma" but nobody in the bar paid the slightest attention. From all appearances, the floor show was going to start in the other corner.

Steve chose that moment to lurch through the door.

Andrea heard the commotion and looked up. For a moment she thought her heart would explode from the way her pulse rate pounded.

If he was glad to see her, his craggy face didn't show it. He took in the status of things in one fast, comprehensive glance around the smoky room. Only then did he desert the doorway and amble across to her table.

"Steve!" She would have hung on his neck if she'd had the slightest encouragement. As it was, she half-rose from her chair.

"Well, baby, I didn't expect to find you here." He made no attempt to lower his voice, but the words came out in a half-slurred drawl. "Tonight must be my lucky night." He shoved Juan's chair close to hers and sank down on it, giving her arm a warning squeeze.

The would-be Romeo at the next table gave them both a disgusted look and grudgingly turned back to his tequila. The other patrons followed suit. A woman alone held in-

126

terest; a woman with a protector . . . They shrugged their collective shoulders.

Steve caught the waiter's attention. *"Cerveza,"* he ordered, flipping the man a coin.

Andrea waited until the other had threaded his way toward the bar before huddling close to Steve and whispering, "I'm so glad you came. Frankly, I was scared stiff."

"Where's Juan?" He barely mouthed the words.

"Gone to take Ellie across the line."

"Hell!"

"But, Steve, she looked ready to collapse—"

"Oh, I know . . . I was afraid she couldn't make it this far. We could use him for reinforcement, that's all." His voice sounded incredibly weary, and for the first time she noticed that he was holding his right shoulder stiffly.

"What's the matter? What happened to you?"

"Keep your voice down," he hissed, "and for God's sake, stop looking like a scared rabbit. You're supposed to be happy to see me." As the waiter approached with the beer, he lolled sideways in his chair, draping his left arm chummily around her shoulders. "Here's what we need, baby." His words came out loud but slurred. *"Cerveza . . .* lotsa *cerveza.* How 'bout another li'l drink for you?"

"No thanks." Thoroughly confused by his manner, she tried to push away. "I don't think you need any more either. And stop nibbling on my neck!" she added explosively.

She felt his shoulders shake with sudden laughter, but he kept his face hidden. "Look, Andy . . . you can protect your virtue another time. Now, pay attention, will you?" He moved his lips deliberately up the side of her neck, keeping his voice muffled. "The main thing now is to try to get out of here in one piece. Take a gander at the doorway, and you'll see there are three brand-new customers."

Her voice was dry. "Pretty soon we'll have a complete service for twelve." She managed to sneak a look at the three men who lounged near the entrance. "Ugh! I'd hate to meet them in a dark alley."

"I didn't care for it myself," Steve murmured, pushing back a strand of her hair and nuzzling her ear. "Fortunately, I ran faster than they did."

Her eyes widened. "That's when you hurt your shoulder?"

"I'm lucky it wasn't my neck. Look, we have to get away from here before they collect any more buddies."

"You mean they're after the money you're carrying?"

"That . . . and other things. I told you there were occupational hazards to this job." He pulled erect long enough to swallow some beer.

"Stop being so cynical."

"Who's being cynical? I'm trying to think of a way to get out of here in one piece. That street outside is dark as a tomb—we'd never make it to the corner."

"I could set a fire in the ladies' room," she offered tentatively.

He looked around. "Where is it?"

Her face fell. "Sorry, this is the wrong bar. I got carried away."

"I was a damned fool to get you into this." His jaw tightened with determination. "You'll stay here; I can draw them off."

"In a pig's eye, sweetie," she murmured. For emphasis, she leaned across, and while pretending to fondle his ear, nipped it sharply. "You haven't a chance of getting out of here alone. I'll scream the place down if you try."

"Don't be a damned fool, Andy!" His angry exclamation stopped, and he rubbed his thumb along the edge of his jaw thoughtfully. "Let me think for a minute."

Andrea was aware of the confusion around them—the hilarity of raucous masculine voices, the out-of-tune guitar, and the clink of beer bottles as the bartender pulled them from a cooler behind him—but she was scarcely conscious of it. The only thing that mattered was the man beside her; it was as simple as that. Later, if they managed to get out of this mess unscathed, she'd sit down and figure out what had happened.

"It might just work," he was saying carefully.

"What would?"

"Screaming the place down." Seeing her puzzled expression, he hunched closer and dropped a light kiss on her bare shoulder.

"I wish you wouldn't . . ." she said feebly.

"That's just the beginning. Look, angel . . . here's how we get out of this place." He was speaking rapidly now.

"We stage one hell of a fight. If anything will bring the police, that will. The owner will be out in the middle of the street screaming for them."

"But who fights who?" she asked ungrammatically.

"You fight me . . . idiot." He glanced toward the sullen-looking men near the door. "I'm not crazy about the other contenders."

"Okay." Her face was so pale that it looked almost luminescent in the murky room. "When do I start?"

"The sooner the better. You're sick and tired of a drunken bum leaning on you—pull out all the stops and chew the scenery. Remember, we need a policeman." At her look of indecision, his jaw tightened. Catching her roughly by the shoulder, he swung her around and fastened his mouth violently over hers.

That drawn-out kiss probed and demanded. It also drained every bit of resistance from Andrea's body. As Steve would have pulled away finally, she instinctively kept her body molded to his.

"Andy . . . for God's sake!" His leathery face was almost as pale as hers when he shoved back with an effort. "You've got the wrong script." The words came out huskily. "You're supposed to clobber me, remember?" He was as oblivious of the onlookers as she was.

The knowledge that she'd forgotten all about the maneuver and revealed her true feelings in a staged kiss made Andrea want to sink through that grimy floor. Talk about idiots! Steve could probably throttle her.

His eyes narrowed, while doing his best to probe her thoughts. "Let's try again," he murmured finally, brushing his lips against her temples.

She pulled away as if stung. "That isn't necessary. Keep away from me."

"That's it," he whispered approvingly, unaware that she was in earnest. He raised his voice. "Don't be silly, baby. Might as well have a li'l fun. . . ."

"You can play games alone." She scraped back her chair. "I'm going home."

"What the hell!" By now Steve was thoroughly confused. "Come back here." Either by design or accident, he put up his hand to restrain her, and it caught in the ring pull of the zipper at her collar.

Andrea felt the material give way on her skimpy bodice

and reacted violently. "How *dare* you! Let go of my dress!" Her open palm came against his jaw with a resounding smack.

Caught off balance, Steve was jarred back, his free hand sending a beer bottle crashing onto the tiled floor.

The splinter of glass acted like the bell at a championship fight. The thwarted lothario at the next table happily lurched to his feet, sending his chair crashing as he aimed a roundhouse right at Steve that would have sent the American halfway to San Diego if it had connected. Fortunately Steve saw it coming and lurched sideways into Andrea, who was so confused she simply followed her natural instincts.

Her first scream cut through the melee and sent the customers at tables nearest the door hurriedly out into the night. Her second scream came after an enthusiastic onlooker sent a tequila bottle crashing into the mirror over the bar. By the time another bottle smashed into the back wall and the guitar was split over the owner's head, half the crowd was involved, and the shrill of a police whistle could scarcely be heard erupting down the street.

When the *policia* came panting in the door moments later, the bar had cleared magically. He saw a room awash with spilled liquor and cluttered with shattered glass. The only people were one man, one woman, and a bartender who was beating his clenched fists on the top of the cash register while loosing a stream of Spanish curses.

Being a wise man, the policeman turned to see if the two customers were worth arresting. His spirits sank after one look at Andrea's blond hair. *Norteamericanos*, most certainly. His enthralled gaze went over her abbreviated frock, which she was hastily pulling into place, and then he turned to Steve. At the sight of that battered individual, the policeman's morale went up. Here was a candidate for the Nogales jail if he ever saw one.

He opened his mouth to speak, but Steve forestalled him. "Do you speak English, officer?" The crisp tones didn't go with the swollen cheek and the puffy eye, which was darkening even as he spoke. Steve saw the policeman's uncertainty and pressed on. "Because it will be easier to explain if you do."

"I speak a leetle, *señor*," the policeman admitted reluctantly.

"Good." Steve was brushing dust from his sleeve. "Would you tell the owner"—he jerked his head toward the man at the bar—"that I will reimburse him for the damage caused tonight, even though my wife and I'"—he ignored Andrea's sudden start—"were not responsible for causing it." As the policeman started to scowl suspiciously at this unwarranted generosity, Steve added, "You understand, *señor* . . . the less publicity for all of us, the better. My wife"—this time he smirked when he said the word, and an understanding glint appeared in the Mexican's eyes—"would prefer it that way."

"Very well, *señor*. I will ask the owner, but you understand, this ees expensive . . . *será muy caro*." He added the last words automatically.

"Of course. I leave it to your discretion," Steve told him.

They watched him stride over to the bar and huddle with the owner, who had started to salvage his unbroken stock.

"Thanks a lot for helping my reputation," Andrea said wryly as she turned to Steve. "Now I know why you wanted me to wear this dress—you didn't have to waste time convincing him. I'll be lucky if I'm not arrested on a different charge." She sobered as she saw him flexing his right hand. "What's the matter? Is anything broken?"

"I don't think so. How about you?"

"I'm all right except . . ." She waggled her ankle experimentally and then bent over to survey her shoe. "The heel's loose on my pump, but I can still walk on it."

"How in the devil did that happen?"

"I think I used it on the friend of the fellow who was hitting you."

"My God . . . where did you hit him?"

"Just on the arm. Somebody else came along then and knocked him down, or maybe that was the guitarist. . . . Things were a little confused. In fact, now that I think about it . . ." Her hand went out to grasp the edge of a table. "I'd better sit down."

"Hey—don't pass out now." He held onto her as she wilted into a chair. "Put your head down between your knees . . . 'way down," he ordered.

Silently Andrea obeyed. Even in her groggy state, the

thought of hitting that floor alongside the broken beer bottles was too horrible to contemplate.

Steve dragged a table closer. "Brace yourself against this. Are you okay? Because if you're not, I'll cart you across the border and then settle these damages."

Andrea did raise her head at that. "You will not. The whole point of this . . . this nightmare . . . was to have an escort to the border. Those goons might still be hanging around."

He waved that aside. "We will have an escort. I'll tell the policeman that you need medical attention, and he can go with us."

"No. Look, I'm all right, so stop hovering." Andrea didn't know whether to laugh or cry at his obvious concern. "It was just delayed shock, I guess. I've never hit anybody with the heel of my shoe before."

"How about the heel of your hand?" he asked, rubbing his chin reminiscently. "You damned near fractured my jaw."

Her eyes went frosty. "Serves you right. I didn't agree to anything like that."

A flush spread over his battered face. "Look, Andy, it was a mistake."

"Your darned right it was!" Her fingers instinctively touched her zipper pull before she went on in an embarrassed tone. "Oh, for heaven's sake . . . go pay the man so we can go home."

He opened his mouth to protest, and then merely nodded grimly and went over to join the huddle by the bar.

Andrea watched miserably while their three-cornered discussion went on and on. Steve must have finally agreed to a figure, because a wad of currency was counted out by the cash register while both Mexicans watched. Then the bartender broke into a grudging smile as Steve reached over to shake hands with him.

After that, there was another discussion between Steve and the khaki-clad policeman. By the glances shot in her direction, Andrea gathered that she was being labeled "unfit for travel." She tried to look suitably infirm, and found it wasn't hard at all.

Finally Steve and the policeman came back to her.

"It's okay, dear," Steve said in his most husbandly

tone, "Officer Sánchez will go with us to the border station. You can lean on both of us."

Andrea nodded and stood up. "But don't you want to stay down and look for Eric?" she asked Steve, suddenly remembering. "He's a friend of ours," she added for Sánchez's benefit.

Steve shook his head warningly. "There's no need. He probably went on ahead with friends, so we won't wait around. Right now I think the best thing is to get back to Tucson. Just hang onto Officer Sánchez's arm on one side, and I'll support you on the other." He tucked his arm familiarly around her waist as he spoke.

Andrea gave the Mexican policeman a grateful smile and then turned to say through her teeth to Steve, "Move your hand, or, so help me, I'll hit you again."

Steve grinned without restraint for the first time that night, and obediently shifted his hand two inches upward. "What's the matter, dear . . . tired?" he asked with a wicked look.

Officer Sánchez glanced at the affectionate clasp and clucked sympathetically. "Ees good to have a man around . . . no, *señora?*"

Andrea knew when she was licked. "Wonderful, Officer. I can't wait to get him home."

Unfortunately, she didn't have to wait until they returned to Tucson to find there was still more unpleasant news in store. Before they left the Arizona border town, they discovered that Juan had taken Ellie to the emergency hospital there.

"The poor kid's a mess," Juan had told them when they met in the hospital corridor. "These last few days with Eric were pretty grim, and then, when she had to see him on the way out with a drug overdose . . ." He shook his head.

"She will be all right, though, won't she?" Andrea asked.

"Physically, yes. Mentally, the doctor says it will take time." He turned to Steve. "I called her grandmother . . . she's on her way now."

The other nodded. "You'd better hang around and see if there's anything you can do to help."

"Okay." The younger man frowned. "I'm sorry as hell about not getting back to you. Did you run into a lot of trouble?"

133

Steve pointedly avoided Andrea's gaze. "It wasn't bad."

"But you got there too late to find our singing bird, I take it?"

"You're right about that. The cage was empty. Eric must have been removed just before I arrived. Somebody left a welcoming committee, but I didn't hang around to fraternize."

"Will you ever find out what happened to Eric? For sure, I mean?" Andrea asked.

"I doubt it," Steve said tersely. "They won't leave evidence lying around down here."

"At least Ellie got out in time," Juan said, "and she's young enough to survive the scars. The devil of it is that we've lost the only decent lead we've had."

Andrea asked Steve about that when they were in the car driving back to Tucson. "What are we going to do now, since this trip turned into a fiasco for you?"

He was concentrating on his driving and replied absently, *"We* don't do anything. You're going home tomorrow . . . remember?"

"Do you have to be so stubborn and stiff-necked about it?"

"Home," he repeated firmly. "You're booked on the eleven-o'clock plane to L.A. Make no mistake about it."

She subsided in her corner of the seat. "Big deal! Just because one trip goes sour—pfft! Out goes the little woman."

"The little woman exits while she's still able to—in one piece."

"And you can go back to researching Françoise, I suppose."

He stared straight ahead. "If necessary. Simmer down and get some rest. You must be tired."

"I feel fine," she said, lying in her teeth.

"I'm glad." He gave her a quick sideways glance then, and his strong fingers tightened on the wheel. "Frankly, I feel like hell, so if we could dispense with this conversation it would be a help."

She was glad the shaded car interior hid her chagrin. All the low blows weren't delivered in the bar in Nogales, it seemed.

"Whatever you say," she managed eventually.

From then on, she stared fixedly ahead, watching the

headlights cut sharply into the darkness of the deserted highway. The little she could see of Steve's profile appeared stern and unyielding.

If he was remembering that kiss in Nogales—as she was—the memory wasn't bringing him any apparent enjoyment. Probably it had been disposed of in the same way he'd efficiently dispatch her to California the next morning. And once out of sight—thankfully out of mind.

There was no reason to be miserable because one overbearing man was sending her away. After tonight, she should be delighted to return to a world of normal people; away from the sordid misery that had haunted her holiday.

And, she might as well face it—Steve wasn't alone in wanting her to leave. Françoise would turn somersaults in the pool, and even Hammerhead would be delighted to see the back of her. The only thing that could carry her lower in the popularity stakes would be a leper bell.

Andrea felt a muscle flicker in her cheek as she bit the edge of her lower lip to steady it. Who would have believed that the prospect of leaving could hurt so much? Or that the memory of a kiss could still stir her senses hours later; a memory so vivid that, even now, she wanted to bury her face against Steve's broad shoulder until he came to life—to love again.

One tear slid down her face and was closely followed by another. She swallowed, being careful not to sniff so that Steve would hear her. It was bad enough to be in love with him . . . she'd be damned if she'd give him concrete evidence.

The car hurtled on through the night. Andrea closed her eyes and let the tears wash silently down.

Chapter NINE

The following morning she was wakened by the ringing of the telephone on her bedside table. Groaning, she reached for it, feeling that she'd aged twenty years overnight. Then, as the bell sounded again, she opened one eye to focus on the face of her traveling clock. Eight o'clock already! She lifted her head and looked toward the draped window, to see a ribbon of sunlight edging the thick material. She shook her head unbelievingly before lifting the telephone receiver.

"H'lo . . ." she murmured throatily.

"Is that you, Andrea?" Graham sounded hesitant. "Are you all right?"

"Just fine, Graham." She cleared her throat and pushed herself up further on her pillow. "To be honest, I just woke up."

"Oh, is that all? I wanted to say that I've arranged for you to be driven into town later on. It's an eleven-o'clock plane, I believe."

"So I've been told."

He missed her deliberate irony. "The airlines people like you to report a half-hour before departure. If Steve collects you about ten, that should give you plenty of time."

"I'm sure it would, but it won't be necessary," she told him sweetly. "Steve must have forgotten that I have a rental car here, and I can manage to get into town by myself. Don't worry, I'll check out in plenty of time for your next guests."

This time her faint touch of sarcasm got through to him.

"Er—yes. I'm certainly sorry that you're leaving, my dear," he told her earnestly. "Steve mentioned you had an unexpected change in your plans. I'd hoped you'd be able to accompany one of our expeditions, but now here you are . . . taking off early."

136

Steve had been busy, Andrea decided bitterly. Aloud she said, "It was most unexpected, Graham. I'm as disappointed as you are."

"Maybe you can come back one of these weekends. . . ." His voice sounded hopeful. "Just let me know, and I'll squeeze you in somewhere . . . even if I have to bed you down in the lounge."

"There's always that bench next to the therapy pool," she said, rallying slightly, "although I'd expect a definite reduction on the day rate."

"You just come . . . we'll arrange something."

"I'll do my best."

"Anyway, I'll see you when you check out, won't I?" he asked.

"Of course. Thanks for calling, Graham." She replaced the receiver and then pushed back the bed covers fretfully.

If Steve thought she was going to forgive him because he'd offered to drive her to the airport, he was sadly mistaken. It wasn't hard to visualize what he planned; there'd be a polite drive to the airport, then a formal handshake when she boarded the plane. She swung her legs to the floor and grabbed for her robe on the way to the bathroom. He'd also thank her on behalf of the U.S. government for helping to accomplish absolutely nothing the night before.

She paused in the midst of brushing her teeth and stared at her reflection in the medicine-cabinet mirror. Why should she think that? She'd accomplished something, after all. She'd shown Steve York how she felt about him in one kiss . . . and the man hadn't stopped running since! If *that* didn't dent a woman's ego, what would? Moodily, she rinsed her toothbrush and put it in its plastic case before tossing it in her suitcase.

She decided on the rest of her schedule while she was taking a shower. She'd have breakfast, check out, and say good-bye to Graham, then drive herself to the airport. There was no need to even see Steve. Certainly he wasn't the type to enjoy lingering farewells. Last night he'd deposited her at the door of the cottage with the air of a man ridding himself of a tiresome blind date.

Andrea made a rueful face in the mirror as she pulled off her shower cap. She might as well acknowledge that

137

she'd struck out completely with the man. Her only hope was that Françoise would find the going equally thorny.

She saw the Frenchwoman sunning on a lounge by the pool as she went in to breakfast. Françoise lifted her sunglasses to peer at her, murmuring a disinterested " 'Allo," and lay back in her chair.

Andrea resisted a sudden urge to push the wheeled lounge into the water as she walked past. The one good thing about leaving, she told herself as she pulled open the glass door to the dining room, was that she was leaving Françoise behind.

To her dismay, she saw that the other half of the Villier family was still at the breakfast table.

Roger rose at her approach. *"Bonjour,* Andrea." He made a dive to pull out her chair. *"Ça va, chérie?"*

She managed a weak, "Fine, thank you," and sat down hurriedly.

"I 'ear you're leaving us. . . ." His accent was thicker than usual. *"Vraiment?"*

"Quite right. Just orange juice and toast, please," she told the waitress. Then, to Roger, "Something came up." There was no need to explain that the "something" was six feet tall and familiar to both of them.

If Roger was suspicious, he didn't let on. "Grandmaw Carter," he said, making a sour face, "she 'ees gone, too. Graham has to forward her things."

Andrea concentrated on the glass of juice being placed in front of her. "Those things happen." She kept her voice casual. "Who knows today what tomorrow will bring? Swinburne said it first." Raising her eyes to meet his, "Or don't you believe in fate?"

He stirred uneasily. "Americans! You wonder too much . . . and ask so many questions."

"A national failing. Eventually, though, we find the right answers. Remember that." She placed the glass carefully back in her saucer. "Are you going riding this morning, Roger?"

"No . . . I 'ave no time," he answered tersely. "There is too much work."

"You should take it easier." She paused deliberately. "Enjoy a sauna now and then."

Her words floated across the tabletop and seemed to hang there.

"I 'ave no time for saunas." He bundled his napkin into a ball and tossed it onto the table before getting abruptly to his feet. "I am sorree you 'ave to go before we got really acquainted, Andrea. A beautiful woman like you should learn how to enjoy life."

His inference was unmistakable. To a European male, a woman's capitulation ranked at the top of the list. Andrea had obviously missed her chance.

She stared up at him. "Why should I take lessons? Most of us want the same things— health, happiness . . . a long life. . . ."

He smiled sardonically. "If that's your list, then it's just as well you're leaving. We look at things differently."

"Miles apart," she confirmed. "But that's what makes horse racing."

He started slightly and then recovered his aplomb. "I wish you *bonne chance,* Andrea."

She reached for the jar of strawberry preserves. "You might need that good luck more than I do."

His eyes narrowed at her expressionless tone. *"Au revoir, m'selle."*

"Adieu, monsieur." She changed the wording deliberately and enjoyed his angry frown before he strode from the room. After throwing down that gauntlet, it was a good thing she was leaving. Probably Roger wouldn't restrict himself to simply locking sauna doors in the future.

She was humming as she left the dining hall after breakfast. The veiled argument with Roger had kept her mind from other things, at least. As she walked to the ranch office, she glanced toward the Rincon foothills. Their profile looked more rugged than ever against the pale morning sky. Thick white puffs of cloud lingered over the higher peaks, but downtown Tucson basked under bright sunshine. She'd miss this marvelous dry weather and the clear desert air. How differently she felt about it now than the day Steve had driven her through the ranch gate for the first time.

Her lips tightened, and she scuffed the toe of her shoe along the gravel path. How often would his name come to haunt her after she'd left the Circle C? Probably too often for comfort, she acknowledged painfully. And the worst part was, the whole affair was so terribly one-sided.

She forced a smile as she saw Graham waiting for her by the office.

"You're leaving a bit late, aren't you?" he asked with a worried look at his watch.

"Am I?" She followed him through the screen door and glanced at the clock above the registration desk. "I guess I dawdled over breakfast. Anyway, this won't take long . . . if you have my bill ready, I'll sign it, and you can mail it to my boss."

He thumbed through the account drawer. "I wasn't worried about that."

"What, then? I'm all packed, and as soon as I sling my bags in the car, I can leave. There shouldn't be much traffic at this time of the morning."

"It's not that. . . ." He shook his head as he pulled a card from the drawer. "It seems like the whole place is in an uproar this morning. I suppose you heard about Grandmaw Carter leaving last night?"

"Roger mentioned it at breakfast," she said non-committally. "He didn't say much."

"Ummm." Graham didn't look up from his column of figures. "She was going to meet Ellie in Nogales. I thought she was visiting somebody in California."

Andrea kept her tone as casual as his. "Maybe she changed her mind. Teen-aged girls do. Let's face it—all women do."

"I know." He turned to run his finger down a list by the switchboard. "You didn't make any long distance calls this morning, did you?"

"Nary a one."

He nodded and went back to the account card. "Didn't think you did." As he bent over his figuring once again, he added, "Well, I'm glad the girl had sense enough to finally steer clear of Eric. He was bad medicine for anybody."

"You talk like he's dead!" She spoke without thinking.

His head came up in surprise. "Did I? It wasn't intentional but I'm not surprised. Addicts don't usually reach a ripe old age." He leaned on the counter. "Anyway, I thought we were talking about Ellie. She could have gotten in real trouble with that no-good kid. The doctors at the hospital warned me when I drove him to town. Human

140

life isn't worth a damn when an addict needs a fix . . . they'll steal, kill, anything you can name."

Andrea was surprised at his vehemence but for the first time she realized why Steve had ordered the young girl across the border so precipitously the night before. Eric's associates evidently made their own rules as they went along. If Eric had talked to Ellie about his suppliers before he had been given the overdose, then her life was in danger, too. No wonder Juan was staying close by!

Looking up, she discovered Graham staring at her intently. She tried to adopt a more casual manner. "Why all this concern about one girl? There's probably a perfectly logical explanation for her being in Nogales." She went on, purposefully vague. "I think Grandmaw said something about Ellie visiting relatives down by the border. Besides, if I know anything about eighteen-year-olds, she's had two or three heart flutters since Eric. Propinquity's the rule at that age."

"It's a good thing." Graham sounded just partially convinced by her argument. "Any girl who mixes with a hophead like Eric deserves exactly what she gets." He grabbed the rolled-up newspaper by his elbow and flattened a fly on the counter with a vicious swat. Then, still clutching the paper, he leaned closer and tapped her on the shoulder with it for emphasis. "All women should be like you, Andrea. Sweet and easy. No secrets—nothing to hide. Everything on the surface so a man knows where he stands." He smiled faintly but his eyes were cold. "It's healthier that way—isn't it?"

Andrea pulled away from him, taking an involuntary step backward as his last words registered. The horror of Nogales seemed to flare up all over again, but this time she was facing it alone. At that memory, the cheerful office surroundings blurred and all she could see was the ruthless look in Graham's eyes.

"Much healthier, isn't it, Andrea?" He kept his voice without expression as he repeated his question.

She shook her head dazedly and then straightened her shoulders with an obvious effort. "Are you trying to scare me, Graham? Because if you are—you're doing a dandy job of it."

"My dear Andrea . . . of course not."

"Good." She clutched her purse tighter. "This morning I'm too tired to fight back."

"I certainly didn't mean to make you look like that." His tone was full of remorse and he rubbed his chin awkwardly. "Lord, I haven't any right to burden you with my opinions and suspicions." He smiled before adding, "I *told* you it had been a bad morning, didn't I?"

The sunlight seemed to flood back into the room at his sheepish confession and Andrea felt foolish for letting her imagination take over—even for a minute or two. No wonder Steve was banishing her from the ranch. After all that had happened, she was as jittery as a beginning driver passing a police car on a narrow road.

"So you did," she assured Graham and smiled in return. "Pay no attention to me. If my bill's ready for signing, I should be on my way."

"There's just one thing more. . . ." He fidgeted uneasily as he completed the bill and shoved it across the counter for her signature. "Steve asked me to hold onto you until he gets here." Graham leaned toward her confidentially. "He was pretty mad when I said you'd turned down his offer of a ride into town."

"That's too darned bad." Her words came out impulsively, and she tried to soften them, when Graham stared in surprise. "Why should he care? I mean, he has so many things to do that I know he can't spare any time." She was aware that her babbling wasn't making much sense, so she made an effort to be concise. "Really, Graham . . . I can't wait around." She patted his hand on the counter. "You *will* let me know when your group is planning a good desert exploration, won't you? I'm sure that I could manage a weekend off to hunt treasure with you."

"Of course. There may be something next month. At the last meeting we decided to explore Carreta Canyon again. One of the fellows has discovered a prospector's map that looks interesting." He came around the end of the counter and walked with her to the door of the room. "I'll drop a note to your office when things are firm."

"Wonderful." She put out her hand. "Thanks so much for everything."

"I should be thanking you," he said warmly, making

142

no effort to let go after the handshake. "Have a good trip, and I'll see you soon."

"Fine." She pulled away gently. "Tell Steve that I just couldn't wait."

"Tell him yourself," came a familiar voice behind her.

"Steve!" The word emerged in an agonized whisper. She put her hands behind her back and started to edge away. "I'm sorry . . . I must go if I get that plane."

"Relax," he said. "I just checked with the airport. The flight's running forty minutes late. We have a few things to discuss first."

Graham frowned. "I don't see why you're so hidebound, Steve. If Andrea doesn't want to wait around—"

"Andrea doesn't know what she wants," the other cut in brusquely. "What I have to say won't take long. We can go in the lounge here."

"You could walk down by the corral," Graham suggested.

Steve stared at him. "For God's sake—why? It's over a hundred in the shade already, and she's not dressed to stand around in the dust." He gestured toward Andrea's linen pumps and knife-pleated emerald-green dress.

"I wish you'd stop talking about me as if I weren't here," Andrea said plaintively. "There's nothing more for us to say."

Graham paid no attention to her interruption. "I thought she could say good-bye to Hammerhead," he explained to Steve. "Women do things like that."

Andrea cut in, "Not this woman. Hammerhead and I aren't on speaking terms at the moment."

"You're right about that," Steve told her. "He'd head for the other end of the pasture if he got a glimpse of you. He still hasn't stopped sulking from the other day."

"I'll bet it hasn't affected his appetite," she said.

"Now that you mention it . . . no."

She nodded grimly. "Just like a man."

"We're talking about a horse," he pointed out.

"*You* may be. . . ."

"I don't know what either one of you is talking about," Graham said, bewildered.

"That's par for the course where this woman is concerned," Steve said, taking Andrea's wrist and pulling her toward the lounge. "If you'll excuse us . . ."

"They're going to be cleaning in there," Graham protested.

"Tell 'em to start someplace else," Steve said before he closed the connecting door from the office behind them.

Andrea pulled free and went over to stand in front of the fireplace, rubbing her wrist where his finger marks still showed. "You don't have to be so brutal. These days a woman isn't dragged by the hair into a cave . . . not if you want a happy ending."

He merely leaned against the door, ignoring her complaint.

"Besides, there was no need for the dramatics." Andrea knew she had to keep on protesting or she'd be sobbing on his shoulder instead. His unwilling shoulder . . . she reminded herself. "You said everything last night. I can even remember the dialogue: 'You've booked on the eleven-o'clock flight . . . make no mistake about it.'" She took a deep breath. "You've made your point, Steve. There's no need to pretend this morning. You won't have to be responsible for me any longer."

He stayed by the door, but she saw him flex the fingers of his right hand into a fist, then deliberately relax them. A small gesture, but it indicated he had nerves like anyone else, and she risked a closer scrutiny. The fine lines around his eyes had deepened overnight, as if he hadn't slept, and his mouth was grim with strain. Something had taken its toll on that impervious personality.

His words showed it still more. "I want you out of this mess," he told her slowly, deliberately, "but I hate like hell to have you go."

"You mean it?" Her lips parted with surprise. "I don't understand," she managed finally. "I didn't help you a bit. Even last night I was just in the way."

"Oh, for lord's sake, Andy—use your head." He moved restlessly over to lean against a glass display case. "Who's talking about work?"

Something fluttered in Andrea's breast, but she kept her hopes under firm control. She did manage a crooked smile. "Well, it can't be my horsemanship. That wasn't much better."

There was a glimmer in response. "Hardly." He paused; then, "You forgot to complain about your nickname.

144

Remember the first day you came? You said that you'd have to be so besotted with a man that you'd lost your reason before he could call you 'Andy'."

"I . . . I don't know what you mean."

He moved slowly over to her and tilted up her chin with one finger. "Don't be a coward now, angel. Not after being so brave about everything else. Don't you know that I've fallen in love with you?"

"Oh, Steve . . ." She threw her arms around his neck and burrowed her nose against his shirt. "You've been such a darned stubborn idiot. I thought I was the only one."

He tugged at the back of her hair so that he could look down into those shining eyes. "If it's any satisfaction, Miss Sinclair . . . you've made a complete hash of my life ever since you got off that train."

"Well, you needn't look so miserable about it," she scolded. "There are some decided benefits to this state of mind, you know."

He shook his head and gently put her from him. "That's the trouble, Andy . . . there can't be any future in it for us. Not now, at any rate. I wasn't going to say anything this morning, but it didn't seem fair to let you go away wondering. . . ."

"But, Steve . . ." She caught him by the arm when he would have turned away. "I don't understand. . . ." Her eyes widened. "You're not married?"

"Of course not. Don't look like that," he commanded in a gruff tone as he reached out and pushed a strand of hair back from her cheek. "Look, dearest . . . you know the kind of work I do . . . you saw last night."

"So?"

"What else is there to say?" His voice took on a hard edge. "There isn't any place in it for a wife and a family."

"Says who?"

"Says me." His jaw was set as stubbornly as hers. "Frankly, I'm a lousy insurance risk. It didn't bother me before, because I hadn't met anyone who . . ."

". . . made you want to change your mind?"

He shook his head. "It has nothing to do with wanting—you know that. But I haven't changed my mind.

You'd look terrible in black, and I'm not setting the stage for it."

She moved toward him purposefully. "Let's put it to the test another way." Sliding her arms around his neck, she added, "If you'd stop talking so much and kiss me instead . . ."

He stifled a groan and pulled away. "Andy, cut it out! That doesn't prove anything."

"Coward!"

"You're damned right. Otherwise, you'd never make that plane, and you know it. When I kissed you last night, I almost forgot what country we were in." He moved over to the door leading to the patio. "C'mon . . . I'll drive you to the plane."

"Steve, you can't mean it!"

"Darling . . . I do. For now, anyway. When you agreed to help us, I told you this was a grim business, and last night should have convinced you. Eric was killed, and we were lucky to get out in good shape. That wasn't an isolated instance; it goes on every day . . . all over the world. For every success, there are a dozen failures. It isn't any life for a woman, Andy, even on the fringes." He raked his fingers through his hair. "We'll have to go now; we're cutting it a bit fine as it is."

"All right." She moved slowly toward him. "I know better than to argue with you. But I'm warning you . . . I won't change my mind, and when this case is over, I'm going to do everything in my power to make you change yours."

The grim line of his mouth relaxed in a grin. "Throwing away the rule book, huh?"

"Absolutely," she said airily. "Just wait until I start my campaign." Moving closer to him, she reached out to twist a button on his shirt. "It's not that you're such great husband material, you understand, it's just that no one got this close to asking me before."

He gazed down into her impish brown eyes and let his glance wander over the beautifully molded cheekbones. "Worried about being a spinster, are you?" he asked with husky amusement. "I can see where you might be."

"Scared to death." She raised her palm as if repeating a vow. "I'm giving you fair warning, Mr. York, you haven't any more hope of succeeding than if I tried to copy one of these museum thingumajigs. . . ." Her amused voice trailed off as she gestured toward the display case.

"What is it, honey?" Steve moved over to where she stood frowning down at the artifact collection behind the glass.

Just then there was a sudden knock on the office door, and when Graham stuck his head around, he saw Andrea in a close embrace with his ranch foreman.

"Oh, sorry," he said lamely. "I didn't mean to interrupt anything."

"You didn't." Andrea pushed away, looking flustered. It was fortunate Graham hadn't seen her fling herself into poor Steve's unsuspecting arms just a second before. Aloud she added, "Steve convinced me that he should drive to the airport, after all. If I changed to a later plane, we could have lunch together. That is, if Steve can have the time off," she wheedled.

"Sure . . . I guess so." Graham looked amused. "I can't remember being consulted about Steve's working hours before." His lips twitched. "I gather that you two worked out your difficulties."

"Perfectly." Andrea gave him a brilliant smile and then turned to take Steve's arm. "Didn't we, darling?"

"Er . . . yes." He picked up her cue. "No problems. It was a silly argument anyway."

"Then maybe Andrea can stay on . . ." Graham essayed tentatively.

"Not a chance." Steve was firm. "I'd never get any work done. Come on, Andrea. Let's throw those bags of yours in the car."

Graham beamed on them as they started for the lounge door. "Well, now I *know* you'll be back for a weekend soon, Andrea. There'll be more than Indian relics on your schedule."

A shy flush wandered over her cheeks, and she complacently surveyed the man beside her. "It looks that way, doesn't it? No wonder people like the Circle C!" She tore her attention away with an effort. "I suppose we'll have to go, Graham. Thanks again for everything."

Steve let the screen door fall shut behind them and marched her out on the path leading up to her cottage before he spoke. "Okay," he said, bending attentively over her, "what gives? You look as if you're about to

147

explode, and don't tell me that it's young love. I know you better than Graham. Keep walking," he added when she would have stopped to explain. "You can talk on the way."

"Listen, Steve . . ." Her fingers bit into his forearm. "For a minute, I thought I was going crazy. I'm still not sure about things, so I thought we'd better pretend. Only it wasn't all pretending, was it?" She looked up at him dolefully.

"Cut it out, Andy." His eyes glinted, but his tone was implacable. "Stick to business. What bothered you in that display case? Was there something missing?"

"Not exactly missing, just different." She tried to match his long strides up the hillside path. "I wouldn't have noticed at all if I hadn't spent so much time in the lounge the other day." She saw him frown, and hurried to explain. "It was the big carved pieces. . . ."

"What about them?"

"They're different . . . not the same ones at all. Where there was a rectangular plaque, now there's a square one. And the silver carving of religious figures has two angels in the corner instead of one."

"That doesn't make sense. It's a permanent collection."

"It's supposed to be."

"Were the placards different?"

"You mean the ones explaining the pieces?" She shook her head. "I don't think so. They didn't have to be, you see. Those pieces today were just a little different, so the written descriptions fitted them just as well. If you're reading an explanation of Indian religious art, it doesn't matter how many angels are on the border."

Steve pulled up as they reached her front porch. "Are you sure you're not making too much of this? Maybe he just stuck in some gift-shop stuff."

"Not with his precious relics. Those substitutions are museum quality, I tell you." She unlocked the door of her cottage. "Come in and look. The piece here on my mantel is sold in the gift shop." She took down the silver-colored bird plaque and handed it to him. "It's nice but not unusual. I saw pieces like it in two or three shops in Nogales."

Steve was looking at the back of the carving. "I know. There's plenty of depth in it for hiding contraband. That's

148

why we went over all of Roger's shipments. We couldn't find a thing." He put the plaque back on the mantel. "What's the story on the museum replicas?"

"All Graham told me was that some selected copies of the genuine artifacts have been made. That's not unusual," she said thoughtfully. "Lots of museums allow that with their prize pieces."

"But if they come across the border addressed to a well-known museum, the border inspection would be minimal." Steve's voice was soft as he frowned with concentration. "All you have to do is hand-pick a messenger to transport the shipments. . . ."

"Eric!"

He nodded. "Very possibly. Furnish him with duplicate invoices so a few pieces of the shipment could be siphoned off before they ever reached the museum. Then store them in plain sight in a dusty lobby display case until the next delivery is made. By God! I think you've done it, Andy. Thank heaven for curious blondes!" He caught her around the waist and swung her high.

She wriggled ecstatically as he put her feet on the floor again. "I'm not sure I like that word 'curious.' "

"How about 'nosy'?" He bent and dropped a quick kiss on the feature in question. "Sorry . . . no time for anything more. Are these two bags all you have?"

She nodded. "Why?"

"Because you're leaving town." He looked around, scowling. "Where's your coat?"

"Darn the coat! I packed it in my suitcase," she told him, following him out to the car. "You mean that you're still sending me away?"

"Uh-huh." He opened the car door and motioned her impatiently in. "Hop it, will you!"

She "hopped it" obediently. He was driving down the road behind the cottage when she spoke again. "Will you have time for lunch?"

"I'm sorry, Andy, but I won't even be able to take you to the airport."

"That's all right," she said serenely. "I'll find the way. What are you going to do?"

"Stop off at the Federal Building downtown. I need all the time I can get. You were pretty convincing in the lounge, but I'm not sure Graham bought the whole thing."

"No wonder he discouraged us from going in that room."

"Not us . . . you," Steve emphasized. "He's probably been switching carvings under my nose for weeks. If we pull this off, how would you like a permanent job in the bureau?"

Her eyes lit up at his teasing. "Hallelujah! I hadn't thought of that. Then I could be under your feet all the time."

He braked at a stop sign and flashed a quick look at her before pulling out on the main road. "You really mean that, don't you, Andy? The sticking-around part?" There was wonder as well as certainty in his deep voice.

Her glance met his squarely. "Of course. I'm just as stubborn as you are, Steve York. Finish your case. I'll wait until you polish off the corners and tie up all the loose ends. No matter how long it takes. All I ask is that you present your final report personally. My boss will know where to find me." She reached out and drew a soft finger down the side of his cheek. "And as our friend Françoise would say, 'I'll be looking forward to it, *mon cher*'."

Chapter TEN

"Now I know what they mean by the term 'elusive woman'!" Steve was protesting two weeks later as he relaxed by the edge of the swimming pool in the brilliant Sun Valley sunshine. "I still don't understand having to track you down here. Why Idaho, for Lord's sake? Or should I be grateful you didn't pick Tahiti?"

"I had my reasons," Andrea said in a demure tone.

Steve turned his head to stare at her, stretched out on the next lounge. He didn't understand that sudden shy note in her voice and manner. It certainly was at variance with her appearance, since she was wearing a turquoise swimsuit which clung so tautly and briefly to her slim tanned figure that he was having difficulty concentrating —even from two feet away.

If he had only known, Andrea's timidity had developed earlier in the day when she'd seen him step out of his car in front of the lodge. Then he'd been wearing a conventional brownish-gray tweed jacket with gray flannels, and from her vantage spot on the front steps he looked tanned, rested, and indescribably wonderful! Now he'd changed to a pair of swim trunks and was his usual informal self, but she still felt unaccountably shy.

She smiled faintly as she stared into the round pool in front of them. Thank heavens, they had the place to themselves for the moment. The younger guests had deserted this smaller, glass-enclosed pool for the Olympic-sized one down by the tennis courts.

Steve suddenly dragged the pad from his lounge down onto the concrete and arranged another one next to it. "C'mon, beautiful"—he caught her by the ankle—"you might as well play Prone Marone as long as we're here. If you're sunning yourself in that rig . . . it doesn't look quite so indecent."

Andrea paused in the transfer. "What are you fussing

about *now*, Mr. York? I bought this . . . rig, as you call it, in the boutique here. It's the latest thing in imports."

"I didn't think it was loomed by the Indians on the reservation," he said wryly. "Somehow it reminds me of a night in Nogales. . . ."

She smiled, her shyness gradually disappearing. This *was* the old Steve, after all. Deliberately, she placed a plastic pillow for her head before stretching out face down with a contented sigh. "The trouble with you," she told him as he followed suit on his mattress, "is that you're old-fashioned."

"Is *that* all? I can remember a time when it took you ten minutes to catalog my sins."

"One of us must have changed," she said happily. She was trying to ignore the breathless feeling caused by his nearness, and had to tear her gaze away abruptly. It would have been safer to linger over a cup of coffee in the lounge with the width of the table between them rather than here—where that tanned masculine shoulder was just inches from her fingertips. She took a deep breath and pushed back on her mattress. This would never do.

Steve had watched the panoply of emotion chase over her expressive features, and smiled slightly. He knew exactly what she was going through, because his own nerve endings were raising cain. So much for his altruistic ideas two weeks ago. All he had to do was get within arm's reach of Andrea Sinclair and . . .

He sighed and reached for a cigarette. "Want one?" he asked Andrea curtly, thinking that if this precautionary measure didn't help, he'd go for a swim.

"No thanks . . . too much trouble right now." A smile played around her lips. "How much longer are you going to keep me waiting?"

His craggy eyebrows went up. "What do you have in mind, Miss Sinclair? This *is* a public swimming area, you know."

She flushed at his teasing but kept her dignity. "Don't be silly; I'm talking about what happened at the ranch."

"Sorry." Obviously he wasn't at all—not with that look on his face. "I must have gotten on the wrong wave length. Besides, it's so peaceful here, I hate to change the atmosphere." He sighed as he surveyed the luxurious surroundings. "You know, this is a great place. It was worth the drive north."

"I thought you'd like it." She watched him light his cigarette and reach for an ashtray. "Let's get it over with . . . then we can forget it."

"And go on to more important things?" He was reading her mind again.

"Uh-huh. There's golf or tennis for later on this afternoon."

"We'll see. Any horseback riding?"

She shot him a suspicious look. "If you insist. I was going to ignore that part of the program."

"Hammerhead sent his regards. . . ."

Her bare shoulders shook with sudden laughter. "You're a terrible liar. Poor Hammerhead . . . he wasn't happy with his lot at the Circle C."

"What do you think about my buying him and sending him to Dad's ranch in Colorado? He'd be knee-deep in clover for the rest of his days."

"Oh, Steve, how wonderful! At least one good thing would come out of all this."

He nodded agreement. "At least one."

There was a pause as she watched him tap cigarette ash into the sand-filled ceramic tray. The muscles in his jaw were taut as he stared at the feathered column of smoke.

"Was it so bad?" she asked finally.

His mouth softened as he switched his attention back to her. "It's never good, Andy. We mess around with a lot of dirty individuals, and soil our hands in the process. I should be used to it by now, I guess." He stabbed the rest of his cigarette into the sand with a forceful gesture. "The worst part comes when you find so-called 'civilized people' right in the middle of the trouble."

"Graham?"

"Yeah . . . Graham Brinkley . . . with a degree in philosophy, an interest in ancient Indian tribes of the Southwest, and a good-paying job."

"Then why, Steve?"

"You tell me." He was fiddling with the belt on her terry robe, which lay folded near her head. "There was a poetic justice about it, though. If Graham hadn't been so dead-set on that hobby of his, he wouldn't have extolled its virtues to you. Then you wouldn't have noticed the switch in the display cases. Or am I doing you an injustice?"

"Not a bit. Usually I stumble around with my eyes half-closed. I'm the least observant person you could have chosen."

"Methinks the lady's too modest."

"And I think you're trying to smooth off the rough edges. What's happened during this past two weeks?"

"First off, the Mexican authorities discovered Eric's body. Their official verdict was a drug overdose."

She winced and compressed her lips. "What about Ellie?"

"According to Juan, she'll be all right, so you can score one for the home team. Her family rallied 'round behind Grandmaw, and Ellie realizes she's a pretty fortunate young woman."

"That's great! Something else for the asset side of our ledger." She paused and shot him a mischievous glance. "Let's go back to the debit side for a minute. What happened to Françoise?"

His eyes glinted with laughter. "Not a thing except that she's busily taking over as temporary manager of the ranch."

Andrea muttered something indistinguishable and then blushed as he laughed at that, too. "It isn't funny," she insisted. "The Circle C will lose all its paying customers."

"Just the feminine ones. Françoise will see to that."

"Hah!" Andrea's snort was scarcely ladylike. "I suppose she gave you an affectionate farewell?"

"Hardly. Not after the grilling we gave Roger."

She pushed upright, unable to contain her excitement. "Then he was involved?"

"Knee-deep," he confirmed, "but not in drugs."

"I don't understand. What about the payoffs . . . the bank accounts?"

"Oh, Roger was making Mexican collections all right —but from a different source. After you'd copied his ledger sheet with the dates and entries, I played a hunch and switched our inquiries from drugs to horses. We scored right away."

"Racing?" She was incredulous. "For pete's sake . . . you mean he was a bookie?"

He chuckled. "It's a good thing that Roger didn't hear you. He'd prefer to be called the treasurer for the family business, but the job hasn't any future. Our government takes a thin view of aliens handling gambling payoffs in this country. My God, we don't even let taxpayers do that. Roger has been told to leave, *tout de suite,* a one-way ticket this time."

"Where will he go?"

"Who knows? Who cares?" His shrug was eloquent. "Want some of this suntan oil on your shoulders?" He was uncapping a plastic tube as he spoke.

"Er . . . no thanks." Andrea knew that if one of those lean fingers touched her, she'd be a goner. It was safer to keep the inches between them. At least for now, she promised herself. Peeping sideways, she intercepted a mocking glance and knew that he was reading her mind again.

Deliberately she pulled her sunglasses from the pocket of her robe and put them on for camouflage. It wouldn't do to have Steve discovering too much, too soon. "Did you ever get Roger to admit that business with the sauna," she asked, striving for a safer subject.

"Nope . . . but he damned well knew what we were talking about." Steve carelessly applied a dollop of lotion to his arm as he spoke. "Chances are that Françoise did the actual honors."

"To discourage my prying around the shop?"

He looked thoughtful as he put the top back on the tube. "To discourage you—period."

"But she didn't even know I'd been snooping." Andrea frowned suddenly, and then her forehead cleared as his evasive comment registered. "Of course, she'd noticed I was trespassing on one of her territories—or making small inroads at least."

"Now wait a minute."

"It's probably happened before," she went on in a reflective tone. "Are you generally surrounded by jealous women?"

"Sure. I fight dozens off every day," he said absently, moving down on his mattress so she wouldn't be in his shadow.

"Then you must use a different technique than you did with me. One hour together, you were ordering me home."

155

His expression sobered. "Finding Eric on the porch of your cottage was the last thing I needed right then. Juan and I had been nosing around for two weeks trying to find his supplier. Without any luck," he added.

"It was Graham, wasn't it?"

"Of course. He used Eric to pick up the deliveries, as we thought. In turn, he satisfied his habit. Naturally Eric wouldn't blow the whistle on a plan like that. The heroin was packed into the back of three or four of the plaques on each shipment. Eric took them to the ranch and delivered the rest of the shipment downtown to the museum for later sales to visitors."

"What happened to the plaques or figures that Graham brought to the ranch?"

"They were stuck in the display case until the buy was made. Simple, ingenious, and very successful."

"Was anyone else involved locally?" Her voice was quiet.

"Just Eric. The trouble started when Graham couldn't keep him or his habit under control. Naturally, Graham told him to sign out of the hospital that afternoon . . . he didn't want anybody talking to the boy. He suggested that Eric head for Mexico until things cooled off. By then Eric had tumbled that he was being aced out of the action. He offered to turn informer because he'd decided our cash payoff was better than Graham's promises. Unfortunately, he didn't live long enough to make the trade."

"Do you think the overdose was an accident?"

Steve rubbed the back of his neck wearily. "Come, now, Andy . . . you don't really expect an answer to that, do you? And what does it matter? He's dead—that's the vital statistic. One potential customer less for people like Graham to supply. Now there's only about a half-million left."

She winced. "What's happened to Graham?"

"The last I saw, he'd been turned over to the U.S. marshal's office. He'll be brought before the magistrate and probably released on bond until his trial. Not only that, he'll be out on parole before you get many more gray hairs." He folded his arms across his chest and smiled wryly. "Sorry . . . I didn't mean to sound like the voice of doom. It's a hell of a problem, and discouraging sometimes—but we try, Andy. My God, how we do try."

There was a moment of silence. Then she made an effort to cheer him. "At least you had interesting side benefits this time. You can't tell me that quizzing Françoise was hard work." She saw the beginnings of his slow grin and pressed on. "Then, there was that first ride you took me on. You really enjoyed your work that day," she accused, "letting me haul Hammerhead out of every edible bush on the desert."

He shook his head sadly. "The trouble is that you have no sense of humor."

"Darned right, I haven't. I'm a scheming, conniving woman," she said, taking a deep breath now that the showdown was in sight. "And I've lured you up here intending to make mincemeat of all your objections to marriage."

"Stooping pretty low, aren't you?" He kept his tone solemn.

She made a sweeping gesture. "Absolutely scraping the bottom. I didn't invite you here because of the climate . . . or the accommodations . . . or . . . anything else," she finished weakly.

"How about indoor sports?" He grinned, reaching for her hand.

"I didn't mean that . . ." she began, and then finished honestly, "But I might try most anything to make you change your mind."

His grip on her fingers tightened at that admission. He let his glance play over her flushed features, as if he were memorizing every detail of her face. Then he said slowly, "I'm not being fair to you, darling—I haven't told you that I've been promoted. Or, at least, pushed upstairs. They've made me a supervisor with a desk at headquarters, and that means my actual field work will be limited. It still isn't the greatest background for marriage, but if you're willing to risk it . . ." His formal mood shattered suddenly. "Damn it, Andy, you will, won't you?"

She pushed her sunglasses up on her head, and he saw that her eyes were shiny with tears. "Oh, Steve, of course! I'm so glad." She shook her head. "Frankly, I didn't know how to start changing your mind."

"The devil you didn't! I should have waited awhile and enjoyed your efforts."

"Beast!"

"You're right." His tone changed, deepened. "You needn't have worried, dearest. You're not the kind of woman a man takes on approval." He gently touched the tip of her small straight nose for emphasis. "You . . . I intended to keep. Right from the beginning. After you smashed my defenses, I couldn't keep you out of my life, so it seemed easier to invite you in. That's where I'd wanted you all along. Right beside me . . . to love and to cherish. Now . . ." He got to his feet and reached for her robe. "Come along."

Still dazed with happiness, she let him pull her up beside him. "Where are we going?"

"Don't tell me that a smart woman like you with her mind bent on seduction"—he was helping her into her terry cover-up and chuckled as he felt her stiffen—"didn't learn some of the other advantages to Sun Valley besides golf and swimming."

She stared up at him, a picture of wide-eyed innocence. "I can't think what you mean."

"It didn't occur to you that there's no residency requirement for marriage in Idaho, and no waiting if both parties are over twenty-one."

"What an amazing coincidence!" she breathed.

His body shook with laughter as he pulled her violently against him. "Andy, you're a terrible liar."

Her arms crept around his neck. "And you're wasting time, Mr. York. Especially when I love you so much."

"Darling!" The brilliant sunshine was blacked out as he bent his head and covered her parted lips.

The kiss began in a gentle exploratory way but changed as their leashed emotions surged to the surface. Both of them were breathing hard when Andrea finally pulled away.

She shook her head, still dazed and trembling. So that was what shared love was like. Heaven, pure heaven.

Steve looked considerably shaken himself. He said huskily, "I'm glad you came up here, after all. Being alone these past two weeks was bad enough, but now that we're together, any more waiting would be sheer hell." His hands moved over her slowly, leaving a trail of fire behind them. "Come on, darling." He caught her wrist. "We have to get changed. That marriage-license office closes at three, and I don't want to be late."

Happiness made her dare to tease. "After that?"

"We'll manage to keep busy."

The look in his eyes and the tone of his voice made her color furiously, but she laughed as she scurried beside him. "Don't worry, Steve, we have a little extra time. When I talked to the license clerk earlier today, she promised to stay open an extra fifteen minutes."

"I know. She told me when I stopped in to pick up the application." His grin flashed as he dropped a quick kiss on her nose. "Andy, dearest, you're a brazen female. I'll have to take you in hand."

"I'm not sure whether that's a threat or a promise, darling," she said happily as they hurried along, "but frankly, I can hardly wait."

SIGNET Rainbow Romances You'll Enjoy

☐ **CARIBBEAN MELODY (Condensed for Modern Readers)**
by Peggy Gaddis. A professional dancer, enjoying stun-
ning success, is thwarted romantically by her partner,
who is determined to keep a beautiful investment from
dancing out of his life into the arms of another man.
(#P5455—60¢)

☐ **ENCHANTED SPRING by Peggy Gaddis.** A beautiful
young girl finds that love can take a perilous course—
even in an **Enchanted Spring.** (#T5137—75¢)

☐ **ROYAL SCOT by Vivian Donald.** It began as a battle to
restore the Scottish monarchy and ended in love and
a flight to the heather. (#P5181—60¢)

☐ **SECRETS CAN BE FATAL by Monica Heath.** A lovely
young girl accompanies a writer to a deserted mansion
to work with him on his next book, not realizing that the
story he is weaving is the bizarre tale of her own past,
a past she has never known. (#P5180—60¢)

☐ **SO NEAR AND YET by Caroline Farr.** A diabolical drama
of hatred and passion is played out at the country estate
of a world-famous ballerina and jungle huntress.
(#P5214—60¢)

☐ **THE QUIET CORNER by Rebecca Marsh (Condensed for
Modern Readers.)** A world-famous actress stalks out of
a Broadway hit and returns home to make the play of
her life—for her sister's fiance. (#P5113—60¢)